USA TODAY BESTSELLING AUTHOR
Dale Mayer

MAN DOWN
TRISTAN

TRISTAN: MAN DOWN, BOOK 4
Beverly Dale Mayer
Valley Publishing Ltd.

ISBN-13: 978-1-778863-34-9
Print Edition

Books in This Series:

About This Book

There is no greater motive than bloodlust, DNA, and revenge mixed up in a cocktail of hatred ...

Tristan had volunteered his assistance to Mason's case, especially as Jasper needs men he can count on. He wasn't expecting to meet the very interesting new coroner, but as the bodies pile up and the mystery deepens, he appreciates her expertise... and the spark between them.

Amarylis had no idea working on Coronado base would be so interesting... or dangerous. Apparently she was watched during her work at the scene of a shooting and picked up something someone wanted... badly.

Now in danger and caught up in Tristan's case, she can only hope he gets to the bottom of this mess before she ends up on her own table...

Sign up to be notified of all Dale's releases here!
https://geni.us/DaleNews

PROLOGUE

TRISTAN MONTGOMERY SAT up stiffly. He hadn't let on that the blow to the head he'd taken two days ago had resulted in a stiff neck and some shoulder injury. He would talk to Pearl about giving him some physical therapy, hoping that she would just wring him out a couple times, instead of making him go to the doctor. Tristan wasn't all that into doctors these days, especially not in hospitals.

They'd spent all day yesterday completing their statements and cleaning up the red-tape mess from the shooting in the ER. It was a good shoot, absolutely no argument about that, but just enough was going on right now that everybody had to make sure the paperwork was dealt with appropriately. Tristan was in the second spare room in Gideon's house, and he walked downstairs slowly.

Pearl took one look at him and ordered, "Sit."

He immediately sat, and she came up behind him and started working his muscles. He groaned with joy, as, one by one, the knots released, and the pain eased up.

"Now go have a hot shower, and, when you come back downstairs again," she said, "there'll be coffee."

He smiled. "How come there aren't two of you?"

"Because one of her is enough to handle," Gideon declared from the kitchen, where he was busy cooking. "And, if you want pancakes, get your ass back down here fast."

"On it, boss." He quickly raced upstairs, feeling so much looser and better after the massage. Pearl had worked his muscles over good, and it made all the difference. After a quick shower, with the heat soaking into his sore muscles, he was soon downstairs and ready for breakfast. When he sat down, Pearl set a plateful of pancakes in front of him. Tristan said, "You don't have to feel guilty and give me preferential treatment for having saved your life. Gideon and Jasper were both at the ready."

"I know that," she replied cheerfully, "but it makes me happy."

"In that case, fly at it," Tristan murmured, around a mouthful of pancakes.

She chuckled, as she sat down and asked, "Who was that nurse by the way?" He looked over at her blankly. "The nurse who was giving you a hard time at the hospital."

He shrugged. "I don't know. Seems like everybody gives me a hard time these days."

"She was cute."

He narrowed his gaze at her. "Oh no you don't."

"Oh no I don't *what*?" she asked, an innocent expression on her face.

"No matchmaking."

"I don't have to matchmake, and she looked positively delighted that I was there, yelling at you."

He snorted. "Yeah, why would someone like to hear someone else getting yelled at?"

"Maybe they're just getting a word in, without being interrupted."

The teasing soon stopped as the three of them dug into

their breakfasts, when Tristan asked, "What about Jasper? Anybody hear from him this morning? He was supposed to call with an update."

"Not yet," Gideon replied. "I suspect he'll be here anytime now. He has a way of showing up when the pancakes are done."

"In that case, we should save him some," Pearl suggested.

Tristan shook his head. "No, we're not saving him anything."

But the door opened without warning, and Jasper stepped inside, sniffing the air. He entered the kitchen and looked at the leftovers on the table and grabbed a plate and sat down. "Jeez," he muttered. "You could have at least told me breakfast was ready."

"Ha," Gideon said. "I figured you would be here anyway."

As soon as he got a couple bites in, Tristan looked over at Jasper and asked, "So, what's going on?"

Jasper sighed. "Well, first off, a nurse at the hospital wants to know how you got released without a doctor's permission and if you're okay. She's feeling quite concerned because she heard what happened." Jasper gave Tristan a big grin. "You better give her a call."

Tristan flushed. "I'll pass. Next?"

"Other than that, we got all the paperwork filed on the hospital shooting. It's been reviewed, and you're in the clear. You're also back to active duty, as long as you feel well enough," he added, critically assessing him.

"Of course I am," Tristan stated, glaring at him. "I barely got hurt."

"*Right*," Pearl noted. "That's why all your muscles were

locked up when you came down this morning, especially your neck and your shoulders."

He stared in disbelief. "I can't believe you threw me under the bus."

"When it comes to matters of life and death, or pain and health, I'll do it every time. You can count on that," she declared.

"Yeah, I do like that about you." Tristan smiled, then looked over at Jasper. "So, where do we stand?"

Jasper gave him a fat smile. "I brought over some very interesting details. So, gather round, and let's get a start on this. Maybe, if we're lucky, we can nail this down and find out who is behind all this, starting with the shooting of Mason."

"I sure as hell wish we knew whether it was a good shot or a bad shot," Gideon noted, looking over at Jasper.

"That's another good point," Jasper replied, "and we aren't likely to know that, not until we get to the end of this."

"I don't understand," Pearl said, not making heads or tails of it. "What do you mean about a good shot or a bad shot?"

Tristan explained, "In this case, a *bad shot* means Drew was aiming to kill Mason but missed his kill shot a bit and just wounded Mason instead. A *good shot* means Drew aimed to wound Mason and hoped to get away with this, free and clear."

"But Drew didn't get away, did he?" she asked.

Tristan nodded. "No, which is why I'll say it was a bad shot, and Drew was killed over it."

"You guys play for keeps, don't you?" Pearl asked.

"No, we don't, but these guys do," Jasper replied, with a

nod. "And, therefore, somebody has to play the game the same way the bad guys do. Don't worry, Pearl," he added. "We're getting a hell of a lot further down the path. We know a lot more than we did before, so we will get this stopped."

"If you say so," she grumbled, with a headshake.

Tristan smacked her hand lightly. "We've got this. Don't you worry. You'll be safe now, and, with any luck, so will Mason and Tesla and Sebastian and Nicholas and Elizabeth." Tristan eyed the last pancake on the table, glanced at the others, decided not to ask, and snagged it right up. "I am the injured one, after all."

Pearl laughed, while Gideon just narrowed his gaze at the empty platter.

Jasper added, "Better eat up, Tristan, because you're next at bat."

CHAPTER 1

TRISTAN MONTGOMERY WALKED into the coroner's office and stopped on the other side of the double doors, staring in through the glass windows. He couldn't see a whole lot from where he stood, but he was waiting to be let in. He was also waiting for Jasper to join him. When he heard a sound behind him, he turned to see a woman walking straight toward him.

She smiled at him. "May I help you?" she asked politely.

"Yes, I'm here to see a body, but I'm waiting for Jasper to get here."

"Ah." She reached out a hand. "I'm Dr. Amarylis Wills," she announced, with the same brilliant smile.

His eyebrows rose slightly. "Now that's an unusual name."

"Not necessarily," she replied. "My father's idea. He thought we were the flowers of his garden."

Tristan grinned at the mocking tone in her voice. "You *are* a beautiful flower, and I'm sure he's very proud of you." She rolled her eyes at the flattery, but he meant it. She was unique, petite, and dark. Her hair was short, almost like a small cap, but it suited her round face and huge expressive eyes. "So, you're the coroner?"

She nodded. "I am, but I'm relatively new here. You probably want to see Dr. Cox."

Tristan shrugged. "I don't care which coroner is on duty," he stated, with a careless gesture. "I came to see the body."

Just then Jasper's voice boomed through the entranceway. "There you are, Amarylis."

She turned and smiled at him. "So, he's waiting for you apparently," she shared, "and here I thought you were never late."

Jasper laughed. "I try not to be late." He quickly made the formal introductions, and she nodded at Tristan. "Pleased to meet you," she murmured. "Now come on in, and I'll show you what you're looking for."

"I was hoping you would have something a little more constructive than just show and tell," Tristan noted.

"That would be nice, wouldn't it?" she stated. "However, if you're expecting results from labs or drug testing, that'll take longer."

"It always takes longer than we like," Jasper reminded him.

Tristan nodded. "We just seem to end up with more bodies than answers, is all."

"Yeah, and you can knock that off anytime," declared the man already inside the room, as they walked toward him. "You know I have plenty of work to do here on my own."

Jasper walked forward and greeted the other coroner. "Dr. Cox, how are you doing?"

"I would be doing better if you quit sending me all these bodies."

"As you know, it's not me sending them," Jasper clarified. "I'm just coming around, asking questions about them."

Cox nodded. "And yet somehow they still all seem to be associated with you."

"Oh, I won't take responsibility for *all* of them," Jasper pointed out, with a laugh, "a few maybe—Tristan as well."

Tristan nodded, as the older coroner glared at him. "What did you want me to do?" Tristan asked, raising his hands in peace. "He was trying to kill me, while they had me locked down in the hospital." Amarylis gasped at that, and he looked over at her. "I guess you didn't hear about that one."

She shook her head. "No. Here in the morgue, we tend to be fairly isolated from those types of stories," she noted. "I can't say I'm against it either."

"Of course not," Tristan agreed, with a smile. "Plus a woman was with me—who had already been through an awful lot—and he was gonna kill her too. So, when he made his move, I didn't have a problem popping him."

"I presume you're responsible for that guy then," Dr. Cox said, pointing to the sheet-covered shape of a body on a table nearby.

Tristan shrugged. "No clue who that one is, but if it's a single bullet wound directly between the eyes," he declared coolly, "that one's mine."

The coroner nodded. "I heard it was a clean shot," Dr. Cox muttered, staring at him.

"It *was* a clean shot," Jasper confirmed, behind him. "As Tristan explained, this guy was set to kill the two of them right there in the Emergency Room."

"Good Lord." Amarylis groaned, her face paling. "We deal with the aftermath, not so much with the process."

"That's probably a good thing too," Tristan added.

"Now, Dr. Cox, what can you tell me about the other guy?"

"I understand you want to see if maybe this body is really Drew Honeycutt. Yet we have Drew Honeycutt's previous autopsy report right here and all the shit that goes with it. So I am doing the autopsy of this body and will compare it to the data on the first Drew Honeycutt. Correct?" Dr. Cox pointed to Jasper, who nodded in acknowledgment. "He also has a single bullet wound to the head."

Dr. Wills turned and stared at Tristan, with a questioning expression.

He shook his head. "Not me," he said, with a smile. "That doesn't mean I wouldn't have popped him too, since we're pretty sure he's the one responsible for the sniper attack that dropped Mason."

She frowned at him. "I did hear about that. … I've known Tesla for a long time."

Jasper confirmed, "We're pretty sure this Drew guy tried to take out Mason."

"Lord." Amarylis shook her head. "And the guy you shot?" She turned to Tristan.

"The cleaner hired to kill all witnesses involved with the same issue regarding Mason," he replied. "We're still trying to get to the big boss who hired all these guys. These are all pretty much just pawns in the game."

"Damn," Dr. Cox murmured. "I don't have a whole lot to tell you about this latest body. He was clean too, as far as I can tell. We haven't got the tox screen back yet, but I'm not expecting to find anything upsetting about it or different. It looks like a clean kill right through the back of the head."

"Execution style?" Jasper asked.

"That's what I would have said," Dr. Cox shared, "but it's almost impossible to tell until you figure out what the hell is going on here."

"As far as we know, and according to the blabbermouth over there," Tristan explained, gesturing to the body of the man he had shot in the hospital, "he was the professional crime-scene cleaner at the house of the woman who was with me at the hospital, that he was so intent on killing too."

The coroner asked, "Not one of my forensic guys?"

Tristan shook his head. "No, he came after you were done collecting evidence. Yeah, this guy was one of the house cleaning crews we normally hired to clean up the mess left behind from the murders, the blood, and all that."

"Jeez." Dr. Wills stared at Tristan. "So, he would have been around there at practically the same time as our forensics people."

"Where this particular guy is concerned—our professional crime-scene cleaner who moonlights as a professional hit man type of cleaner—I think he was probably lurking around every scene. He was definitely inside when the woman's house was being professionally rid of blood." Tristan nodded. "We think he was in the area when the intruder was shot at the woman's house too. That same woman was at the hospital with me, and this guy wanted to shoot us both because it involved her house."

Amarylis frowned at him. "There seems to be an awful lot to this story that you're not telling us."

"An awful lot is involved leading up to this story," Jasper noted cautiously, "and honestly? The less you know, the better. Most of it needs to be kept under wraps anyway."

She shook her head. "It's awfully hard for us to do our jobs if we don't get full access to all the information."

"That's true," Jasper conceded, "but, if for any reason the bad guys decide to kidnap you, and they think that you have information they want—or don't want you to have—wouldn't you prefer to *not* know?"

She stared at him, her gaze intent. "That is one theory, but, if I don't know anything, I have nothing to give them and nothing to save my life with. They will think I do have the information regardless."

"But, if their *belief* is all they need in order to take you out," Jasper shared, "it won't matter what you say. Can't argue with them, when killing people solves all their problems, or so they think."

She shrugged and nodded. "I still would prefer to have the whole story."

Dr. Cox looked over at her intently, "I have most of it," he stated, his tone harsh and brash. "I'll fill you in afterward."

She nodded. "That would be good." They continued to discuss the male in front of them, and, when they were done, Tristan looked over at Dr. Cox.

"Now the woman's body," Dr. Cox indicated, with a sigh, as he looked over at Amarylis. "That is one of yours."

"The woman who was brought in this morning?" Amarylis asked.

Dr. Cox nodded. "She is related to this whole mess too."

"Jeez." Amarylis quickly walked past several other tables to reach another figure, lying on the far table. "How does she fit into this?"

"She's the one who clubbed me over the head," Tristan declared, his voice turning harsh, "putting me in the hospital. Then the same guy who tried to take me out at the hospital is probably the same one who took her out beforehand. He's cleaning up loose ends."

"Nice world you guys live in," Amarylis muttered.

"No, not at all," Jasper argued, "but Mason's case is the world we have to deal with right now, so we don't have a whole lot of options."

"I get it," she admitted, while scrunching up her nose. They quickly went over the details on the dead woman. "Honestly, this one died long before her time. She was in her mid-fifties, in good shape. She was healthy, no sign of any disease in her body. She was a nonsmoker, and everything looked good, except for the bullet wound to the side of her head," Amarylis shared, looking back over at Tristan.

"I didn't shoot her. However, just in case you're worried," Tristan teased, "a bullet between the eyes is standard practice for any of us who were trained to shoot properly. If you don't know how to shoot, then you aim for a chest shot. That way you're more likely to hit your target and to bring them down. You can always finish them off after that." Amarylis gave a stifled groan, but Tristan kept going. "Yet those of us who can shoot and can hit our target, we take them out with a head shot. It's faster and cleaner."

She winced and nodded. "So, you're not the only pros on this one. But she likely moved right as he shot."

He smirked, wondering how a coroner could have qualms about all this. "Considering you probably don't understand a job done by a rookie versus a pro in this context," he noted, giving her a boyish smile, "you're right."

"What did I say wrong?" she asked in confusion.

"What we're dealing with in this case," Jasper jumped in, "are actual mercenaries."

"Ah." She shook her head. "That's even uglier, isn't it?"

"Exactly," Tristan agreed. "It is ugly when somebody hired these guys to try to take out Mason, and some of these bad guys probably knew Mason on a personal basis, particularly Drew here," he added, pointing back at the cadaver they'd just been looking at. "Drew was military and had worked on this base for many years. No way he wouldn't have come into contact with Mason at some point."

Amarylis frowned and suggested, "Maybe that's the source of the unrest?"

"Maybe, but there's just not enough of an evidence trail to show that," Tristan replied. "What I do need is everything you can tell me about the female. She appears to be the weak link here."

"In what way?" Amarylis challenged.

"She left me alive, for one," Tristan responded, looking at Amarylis directly. "So she's not as bloodthirsty as the rest of her team. However, that reason alone got her killed for her deemed failure on the job."

"God," Amarylis muttered, shaking her head. "Okay, fine. I don't have a whole lot on her though, but I'll run you a copy of what I have."

"Send it to my email, please," Tristan stated.

"I'll send it to all of us via email," she muttered. She looked over at the head coroner, and he just nodded.

"You do that," Dr. Cox confirmed, with a nod. "Everything that's just been discussed here is otherwise under wraps," he added. "So we don't talk about it with anybody else but the approved military investigators."

"Unless of course we're brought in for questioning over it," she added.

Dr. Cox added, "In which case these guys will be there too."

"Good enough," she said cheerfully. She headed out of the main area of the morgue, and Tristan watched as she went into a small room off to the side.

Dr. Cox smiled. "Dr. Amarylis is new, but she's sharp as a tack."

"She appears to be," Jasper noted.

"She doesn't necessarily know how things work when you guys come around, though," Dr. Cox noted.

Tristan gave him a hard smile.

Dr. Cox shook his head. "That's okay. She'll learn."

Tristan burst out laughing at that. "Does this mean that you're leaving us, Doc?"

"No," Dr. Cox declared. "It's just that you guys keep bringing me more than enough business, and I needed some help. I did have another doctor doing his practicum here, and we were looking to keep him on, but he decided, well, he didn't want to work here with me." Dr. Cox shrugged.

"Sorry about that," Tristan replied. "It's always tough when you can't find decent staff."

"It is, indeed." Then Dr. Cox smiled. "Lucky for me, Dr. Amarylis came along."

"LUCKY FOR YOU, indeed," Amarylis confirmed, as she walked back into the main room, smiling. "Not everybody wants to deal with dead bodies and murders all day long."

"How can you be a coroner and *not* deal with murders?" Tristan asked her.

She smiled at him. "There are all kinds of places in the world where murder is not the prevalent mode of death. I wasn't even thinking it would be here," she admitted, as she shook her head. "But, hey, I came from Chicago, and it's pretty damn hard to beat those kinds of numbers."

"What brings you here?" Jasper asked, eyeing her intently.

She stared at him for a moment and finally spoke. "A change of scenery, a change of pace, wanting to do something that helps our guys." She shrugged. "Any and all of the above. I gather I'm under suspicion now?"

"You're not under suspicion as much as you're new, and that means we have to look at you sideways for a while."

She laughed. "That's okay. You do what you have to do." She handed them both the paperwork she had just printed out. "I already sent these to your emails as well."

"Good enough." Tristan nodded.

She watched them as they headed to the door. "No more bodies today, *huh*? We're a little busy."

"Got it." Tristan smiled. "I'll try *not* to add to your workload." And, with that, he was gone.

Amarylis still watched as the door swung shut behind him.

"That's an interesting reaction," Dr. Cox noted at her side.

She turned and asked, "What is?"

"*You*," he said, with a nod at the closing door before them.

She shrugged. "It's interesting to see the men causing all this ruckus."

"Not *causing* it," Dr. Cox corrected. "You'll see a lot of the men who have pulled the trigger here, depending on various situations, … but they're not the cause of it."

"No, of course not." She said, raising her hands in defense. "Sorry, I didn't mean to suggest that they were murderers or anything like that."

"Good," he noted, with a warning in his tone, "because that will never go down well on a base like this."

"I'm just not used to seeing killers, and here are these men who put the bodies on my table, just walking around like that."

"Did you not ever deal with the Chicago cops involved in shootings?"

"Most of the time they were pulled off duty after each incident, so they weren't the ones we dealt with," she explained. "I can't think of too many instances, if any, where I had something like this happen."

"Get used to it," Dr. Cox stated, with a nod. "These guys are naval investigators, and they deal with some of the toughest aspects associated with our military bases, both domestic and overseas. They can be sent anywhere, depending on the trouble that they're dealing with."

"That can't be easy either," she muttered, shaking her head.

"No, and most of them are damn good guys, but that lifestyle, that living, takes a toll after a while," Dr. Cox shared, staring at the door. "Anyway, we need to get moving. If you get any other results back, send a copy to me and to them."

"Good enough," she replied, leaving the room again. For the rest of the day it was business as usual. As she worked, it was hard to get Tristan off her mind.

Jasper was almost equally disturbing, but in a different way. An attraction was there between her and Tristan, and Amarylis didn't want it to be anything to do with the work they did. That just sounded so wrong, and it came from a part of her history that was holding her back. Yet she didn't see anything happening between her and Tristan. She'd dated plenty of guys who were either turned off or completely turned on by the work she did. In this case, she didn't see any of that happening here at this base, and that was a good thing.

She walked out of the offices later that day. She was still getting used to the base, and she was getting there slowly but surely. As she walked to her car, she heard a shout and turned to see a man walking toward her, one she didn't recognize. She frowned, hesitating, not sure she should talk to him.

As he stepped up, another man stepped out from the shadows and called out to her, "Hey, honey. Sorry, I'm a bit late." She startled at that, recognizing Tristan. Her eyebrows shot up, and he just gave her a warm smile as he walked closer. He turned and looked at the other guy. "Do I know you?"

The other guy frowned and shook his head. "*Nah*, I didn't realize she already had a boyfriend. You know how hard it is to meet anybody in this damn place? I figured, because she's new, she wouldn't have hooked up with anybody yet," he said, growling.

"Ah, that is so sweet of you, wanting first dibs, *huh*?" Tristan taunted him.

The stranger turned all shades of red and faced Amarylis, adding, "Anytime you want to ditch this clod, you give me a call." Then he quickly handed her his phone number on a card.

Stunned at the speed in which the circumstances had just evolved, she waited until the other man disappeared, frowning at the card. "*Garran*. What do you know about Garran that you seemed to think I needed saving from?"

"I wasn't so sure you needed saving at all," Tristan stated, "but what I do know is that, until we get to the bottom of this shooting-Mason mess that we're in, everybody involved needs to be careful."

She frowned. "Yet how do you know that I didn't want to go out to dinner with him or something?" she asked, her gaze assessing Tristan.

"Because you didn't know him and instinctively didn't trust him," he replied. "I saw that from your expression and your body language. Besides, I reacted on sheer impulse and called out to you."

Her eyes opened wide. "Do you often do things like that?"

He shrugged. "Sometimes instincts are a huge boon."

"It can also get you in a hell of a lot of trouble."

He burst out laughing at that. "It can, but, given the amount of trouble we've got going on right now on this base, I didn't want to take the chance."

"There is that," she agreed. "Do you know who that guy was and what he was doing here and whether he was looking for me or not?"

"He was coming for you. Whether that's because you are fresh blood on base," he explained, "or you just took up a position in the coroner's office, it's hard to say."

"It sounds terrible when you put it that way."

"Sorry, didn't mean it to, but I'm a straight shooter. Plus, I'm not prepared to see anybody else get hurt, especially since we already have several bodies in your morgue."

"What about Dr. Cox's safety?" she asked.

"He was escorted home earlier," he shared.

Her eyes squinted at the word *escorted.*

Tristan shrugged. "Jasper had a guard on him, but we didn't realize you were staying on so late tonight."

"So you got the unlucky card?"

"I would say, I got the *lucky* card." He chuckled. "Besides, if you want to go out with *Garran*, we can call him back right now. Or you can call him. You've got his number right there."

"He was a little pushy, wasn't he?" she asked, frowning as she stared again at the card.

"I don't know." Tristan shrugged. "From a guy's point of view, he was just getting in line first. He probably thought I might take things over."

"Would you? Would you just take things over?"

"Of course not." He chuckled, as he nudged her toward her car. "I would give you an option first."

She sighed. "I'm here at my car, so now what?"

"Now you will go straight home," he said, rolling his eyes.

"What if I want to go out for a meal because I don't have any food at home?"

Tristan stopped and whistled. "How new are you here?"

"Two weeks," she said. "Sure, I've done some shopping, but I don't have a fully stocked kitchen yet. Plus, I haven't figured out where all the best food places are."

"Oh, I can help you out with that," Tristan offered. "Considering I just made it appear as if you and I are together, it wouldn't hurt to show anybody else who's watching that we're a couple."

At that, she faced him. "Is this all just for show?" she asked. "Is this what you do?"

"If I have to do something to keep you safe," he replied, with his wolfish smile, "then I'll do whatever it takes."

She shook her head. "This isn't what I signed up for."

He gave her a grim look. "None of us signed up for a military sniper taking down a beloved leader like Mason. But, when trouble finds you, you can't sit around and do nothing."

She winced, and his saying how he hadn't signed up for this either stuck out like a sore thumb. "Meaning that *you* didn't sign up for this either."

"Meaning that I didn't either, and neither did the other women involved," he added, "like Tesla."

Amarylis nodded, now frowning.

"Didn't you say you know her?"

"I do know her. I've talked to her a couple times since I arrived here, but I have not gone to the hospital to visit her."

"Has she asked you to?"

"No, she knows how I feel about hospitals."

He frowned at her and asked, "Seriously? You work in a morgue, for heaven's sake."

"Exactly," she agreed, "and, all too often, the people I see in a hospital, they end up in my morgue. I would just as soon not see them in a hospital. If they show up dead on my table, well, that's something I couldn't help. Yet, if I've seen them in the hospital first, I always worry I could have done something more for them."

He gave her the gentlest of smiles and nodded. "And yet that's not your field, is it?"

"No, it sure isn't," she agreed, "but that doesn't mean I feel the pain any less."

"No, of course not. That just means you're all heart."

"*Too* much heart," she muttered, with a headshake. "Such a sensitive heart can make life pretty tough."

He smiled. "Absolutely it can. However, I won't say it's a bad thing because I think there's a lack of heart in this world."

She nodded. "I won't argue with that either."

"Good. Now that we've got that out of the way, let's go

eat. I know a place just down the road. Do you want to drive, or do you want me to follow you home, and then I'll pick you up from your place? Or we can leave your car here, and I will bring you back afterward." When she hesitated, he added, "You know that I'm trustworthy. You also know that at least two others are aware that I'm assigned to you tonight, including Dr. Cox, so you also know that I'm safe."

"Why do I feel like there is more to this than just a dinner?"

"Right now, before there's any trouble, we just want you to be safe and sound," he explained. "It's always calm before shit just gets sprung on us. I would feel a whole lot better if you had somebody you could call on."

"Wow." She let out her breath with a heavy gust. "This is definitely not the reception I was expecting here."

"No, but the minute you got those bodies on your table, who knows what will happen."

"Do you think they will come after the bodies?" she asked, as she got into her vehicle and closed the door, rolling down the window now.

"I don't know that they will come after the bodies, but they might come looking for more information." He shrugged because what more could he say? She was already reeling. "I also wanted to ask you privately if you saw any sign of either of them being a drug mule."

"Good God, I didn't see any sign of that. I did a full autopsy and found no packets in the stomach or intestines, nothing in that area that would indicate something like that." She was clearly unnerved by now. "I've certainly done updated training, and the drug trade is always trying new things. However, only so many body cavities exist where they can hide drugs."

"I get that. I just wanted to confirm, that's all."

"You couldn't have asked that this morning," she noted, with a note of humor.

"If I'd thought of it then," he admitted, flashing her a grin, "I would have. Now, what's your choice?"

"Meaning I don't have a choice, or I do have a choice of transport or regarding dinner?"

"Yes, of course you have a choice," he said, rolling his eyes. "I can escort you straight home, if that's what you want, or we can go out for a meal, or I could just shadow you while you go do your thing."

She turned on her car engine and asked, "Do you seriously think I'm in any danger?" When he hesitated, she added, "What are you not telling me?" He stared at her and didn't respond right away. She shook her head and spoke impatiently, "What is it?"

TRISTAN WAS GOOD at casual, but he was no hand holder. Yet he couldn't see the point in scaring her.

"Come on. You need to tell me. If I don't know what's going on, I can't protect myself."

He nodded. "That's part of the problem. I don't know why anybody would want to come after you," he replied, raising his hands, stopping her before she opened her mouth again. "I just know that it's a possibility, and my instincts are telling me to keep you safe. I don't want to scare you or to freak you out. I'm here unofficially, yet I also followed Dr. Cox home today to ensure he got there safely."

"Did you talk to him?"

"I did," he confirmed, with a nod. "I gave him a full

warning that … this case is ugly and that he needs to take extra care."

"You've got to be kidding me."

"No, I am not. He has no family and lives alone," Tristan shared.

"And so do I," she noted. "Is that a good thing or a bad thing?"

"It's hard to say, but, should you unwillingly disappear, not a whole lot of people would know immediately. And maybe, from the bad guys' point of view, not a whole lot of people would care."

She paled as she glared at him. "Sounds like scare tactics."

"It is, and I'm known for being overly cautious. I get it. However, I also want to see that this mess doesn't have anything to do with you."

"You're still not making any sense as to what connection there could possibly be to the coroner who's looking after these cases," she pointed out. "I get that you don't want to tell me, but we're not going anywhere until you do."

He grinned. "I do like feisty people."

"You mean, feisty *women*," she clarified, raising an eyebrow.

"That too," he agreed. "The thing is, I don't have any proof for you, but I can tell you that I'm very well known for my instincts, and right now my instincts are telling me that whatever is going on in that morgue with those bodies is bad news for you, and I would just as soon keep you out of it."

Before she could open her mouth in protest, he added, "You don't have to agree, but the mistake of not listening to me could have huge consequences." She glared at him, and he nodded. "I know it's not fair, and I don't have anything concrete to tell you. All I can say is that something's wrong, and I want to confirm you're safe. Is that so hard to believe?"

"If it wasn't for the fact that Dr. Cox and Jasper were here earlier, I would think that you're on the same level as the Garran guy who just left," she pointed out, staring at him.

"You don't think it's odd that he was waiting right here in the parking lot for you to leave?"

She nodded. "I think it's very odd, but, honest to God, since everybody got loose from COVID restrictions, there's been a lot of odd and desperate people, wanting to hookup, to make friends, to get out, and to just have a life again, you know? So, is it odd? Sure, but it's not the oddest thing I've had happen."

"What was that?"

She shrugged. "A couple days ago, I came out of my apartment, and somebody was staring at me the whole time. I smiled at him and was friendly, but he was just very strange." When Tristan raised one eyebrow, she got nervous. "Oh, surely that's nothing to be upset about."

"I guess it depends on the guy. Does he know what you do?"

"He did ask me what I did and if I was new here and working and all. When I told him that I was the new coroner, he nodded. Although," she added, with a wince, "he did say, *too bad.*"

"*Too bad,* as in he didn't want anything to do with you because you were a coroner, or *too bad,* as in too bad for you?"

"I don't know," she admitted, staring up at him, "but now you've got me wondering."

TRISTAN FOLLOWED HER back to her place, and as soon as they got into the apartment parking lot, he pulled ahead and parked, then got out and walked toward her. "Would you recognize this guy again?"

"Sure, he had a fairly distinctive expression on his face when we first met, so I had a good look at him."

"What kind of expression?"

"Like I surprised him."

"I'm guessing you probably did. Not everybody sees a *pretty young thing*, like you"—deliberately drawing it out in a joking manner—"as being in *that* field."

"Not the first time I've dealt with that discrimination," she admitted, "and sometimes this work gets me into trouble in terms of relationships."

"Of course," he murmured. "Do you think the guy lived here?"

"Maybe, I don't know. Why?"

"I just wondered." He turned around, looking at the apartment buildings. "I would like to know who you were talking to."

"He was leaning against an older black truck, though I don't know anything about trucks," she shared apologetically. "So I can't tell you what kind or model it was. I can tell you that he had a scar down the right side of his face."

"Did he appear to be waiting for you or in any way interested in you?"

She winced. "You know how to make a girl feel special."

"What I want to know is if somebody is interested in you *for you*, not because you might have been seen somewhere."

"Where would I have been seen?"

"I don't know. Were you at any of the crime scenes?"

She grimaced and then nodded slowly. "Yes, of course. It's part of my job."

"Exactly, and that's why I'm asking. I'm not sharing this to scare you, but I do want to know more about whatever is going on, so we're very clear as to what it entails."

She sighed and raised her hands, and he ushered her to his car. "It's frustrating, and I have zero clarity to give you."

Just then his phone buzzed. He pulled it out, checked the screen, and nudged her toward his car as he answered the call. "Hey, Jasper. … Yes, yes. I did drive behind him. … I know, overly cautious and all that. Yet Amarylis here, .. yeah, Dr. Amarylis Wills," he clarified quickly, wincing at the overly familiar tone that she hadn't told him that he could use. "She's had two guys focused on her. One guy in her apartment parking lot seemed to be staring at her, who made an odd comment about how bad it was *too bad* that she was a coroner. Maybe it was innocent, maybe not. I don't know." He looked right at her and nodded. Then Tristan went on to explain about Garran, the latest guy who had rushed up to talk to her tonight as she left the office. "I was just asking her if she had been at any of the Mason-related crime scenes."

She half listened, as she thought about it. When he got off the phone, she added, "I was on scene, picking up Drew's body. Then I was sent back out to collect your mystery woman."

Tristan nodded. "Do you think you were being watched either time?"

"I don't know. I wasn't alone each time though."

"I don't suppose you noticed anybody who showed up at

both scenes, like a civilian or someone not official?"

Her eyes widened at that. "Again I have no idea. I don't know anybody here."

"That's partly why I'm concerned." Tristan surveyed the area. "Let's go get some food, and we'll talk about it."

As he got into the driver's seat, she noted, "I don't understand what could possibly be an issue."

"An issue would be if you picked up something at a crime scene that the bad guys know about and were hoping to get themselves."

"But then it would be back in the morgue, with forensics, and part of the inventory."

He nodded. "How much security do you have at the morgue overnight?"

"I don't know." She shrugged. "That would be a question for Dr. Cox. I'm still pretty new here."

"Will do." He drove down a series of roads and came up to a small restaurant she hadn't seen before.

"What is this place?" she asked, staring at it.

"It's Italian, a small hole-in-the-wall place. Do you like Italian?"

"I love Italian," she replied, with a smile, "and I always love hole-in-the-wall places." She laughed. "Anything that makes the food a little more family-oriented."

"That's definitely this place," he stated. "Come on. Let's go get something to eat."

As they got out and walked into the restaurant, he quickly introduced Amarylis to Rosita, who was serving tables.

Rosita smiled at her. "Welcome to town," she greeted her in a cheerful manner. "Let's grab you guys a table."

As they walked to the table, he felt Amarylis's gaze on him, and he shrugged. "I come here sometimes. I know the family."

"She seems to know you quite well too," she teased.

"I don't know about her knowing me *well*," he clarified, "but I helped her brother when he was in a spot of trouble."

"Ah, back to the Good Samaritan thing."

"Not sure I do that whole Good Samaritan thing very well," he murmured. As Rosita pointed them to their table, he said, "Thanks, Rosita."

"Do you want the usual or menus?"

"As this is Amarylis's first time here, let's not push it, so how about menus?" Rosita nodded and quickly disappeared. He looked over at Amarylis and asked, "What's the matter?"

"I'm just wondering about something," she replied. "You know when you mentioned picking up a few things?"

"Yeah. Did you go through Drew's clothing?"

"I didn't. We're not fully done, remember that."

"Forensics isn't done either," he noted, "but it does make me wonder."

"I did see something and picked it up. I'd forgotten about it until now."

"What was it?"

"A key."

He looked at her over the top of the menu. "As in a USB key or a door key?"

She nodded. "A USB key. It went in with a bunch of other items to forensics. They would have it on record."

"So, you're not handling that part yourself?"

"No, a forensics team goes to scenes here, particularly right now," she explained, with a shrug. "I don't know if there always is one. On several of my Chicago jobs, I gathered forensics as well as managed the forensics team, but that doesn't appear to be part of my job here."

He nodded. "No, we have a full contingent here, so chances are it won't be your job."

"But not everybody would know that," she pointed out.

"Meaning that anybody who saw you pick up the USB, or thought you might have picked it up, wouldn't know that it wasn't your job?"

"Exactly, so, in theory, what you're saying about me potentially being in danger is a real possibility." She put her menu down with a hard slap and glared at him. "And I won't thank you for that because now it'll be damn hard to sleep."

He studied her features. "Still, we're always better off knowing, so we can do something about it."

"Says you," she muttered. "I'm beginning to feel like I've walked into *Alice in Wonderland*, you know? Right down the rabbit hole, with absolutely nothing good about it."

"We can certainly make some phone calls and see what's happening with that key."

"That would be good," she stated in a hard tone.

"Who did you give it to?"

"It went into an evidence bag and was handed off to the forensics team. I don't even know if anybody recognized it for what it is."

"In what way?"

"It didn't look like a typical key. You know how you have all these novelty designs and things?"

"So, if nobody recognized it, then how did you spot it?"

"This one was in the shape of a little car. My father sold a lot of computers and accessories, and he used to give away promo stuff like that all the time to his clients. When I picked it up, I knew what it was. I didn't open it or even look at it very long, but I did put it into evidence."

"So, as soon as we're done with dinner, maybe you can

make a few calls, and we'll see what is on that key."

"The lab guys don't work twenty-four hours a day," she said, looking at him.

"Unless they need to, and, if I need them to, then we will get them in there."

"Oh, crap." She gave him an eye roll. "You know how to make me popular, as the new person on the block."

"Oh, don't worry about it." He waved his hand. "I'm always happy to be the bad guy. You can blame it on me."

She burst out laughing, just as Rosita walked over to take their orders.

CHAPTER 2

AMARYLIS KNEW TRISTAN was chomping at the bit to have her call forensics. She wasn't sure what the protocol was. So, since she was new and didn't want to get herself in trouble, that was not an easy decision for her. Yet, if something needed to be looked at, it was the job, and she needed to figure it out. She quickly phoned her boss first, and, when Dr. Cox answered, she explained what the problem was.

"Call them in," he urged. "On something like this, you always want to keep on it."

"That's not going to sit well with them."

"Most of the time we don't have any issues, but this is a strange case, with a high body count," he pointed out, "so let's do whatever we can."

"Are you aware that Tristan followed you home tonight?" she asked Dr. Cox, looking directly at Tristan.

Dr. Cox laughed. "Yeah, he wasn't very subtle about it."

"Wasn't trying to be," Tristan replied, loud enough to be heard.

Amarylis groaned and put it on Speakerphone. "That's him yelling at you."

"Oh, where are you guys?" he asked in a surprised tone.

"He's insisting that I look after myself," she muttered. "We had a strange encounter with somebody outside the office."

"I don't know what strange encounter it was," he noted in alarm, "but don't take any chances. As long as this Mason case is going south, we want to ensure that we're north of it."

She thought about all the things he could have said and asked. "Is this part of my job?"

"Being new, you're not used to working in this environment. You're probably not used to working where your ass will be put on the line." He took a moment and added, "Normally I can't imagine that being the case, but, for whatever reason, we appear to be caught up in something unusual right now. So, if you did see something like a USB key going through the system, we do want to confirm that it won't go missing."

"Right, so do I phone forensics?"

He thought about that for a moment, as the silence stretched. "I'll do it. Let's keep your head off the chopping block as much as possible." And, with that, he hung up.

She looked over at Tristan. "Happy now?"

"Happy enough," he replied, with a smile. "As Dr. Cox said, we don't want your head on the chopping block, but neither can we afford to let this slide."

"I wasn't thinking we were letting anything slide. I gathered evidence and handed it over as usual, pretty sure it would get processed along with everything else."

"Under normal circumstances it absolutely would be fine, but you gotta remember"—and he leaned closer now—"that your two interested males seem to be military personnel. So, if they were looking for something in particular and thought that maybe you had it or that it was picked up, there's a good chance they would think you have it or you would know where it is."

"I don't need that as a sleep aid either," she muttered.

"No, of course you don't, which is why we're doing what we can right now to fix this."

It wasn't long before the deep-dish pizza they had ordered arrived, and, on the heels of that, Dr. Cox called her back and greeted her with "Put it on Speakerphone, please." She did so, and they both leaned forward to listen to the coroner. "Tristan, I contacted the lab, and they say they didn't see any key."

"And yet I did put it in an evidence bag," she pointed out.

"But you also mentioned that it might not be something everyone would easily recognize as a USB key," Tristan reminded her.

"I want you both, when you're done with whatever you're doing there, to meet forensics at the office. I've got John heading over right now."

"Do we get to finish eating first?" Tristan asked, with a note of humor. "A lovely deep-dish pizza just arrived."

Dr. Cox snorted. "You better get it to-go then. Once you start this process, it happens, and fast."

What surprised her afterward was how quickly they were suddenly standing outside her office building. She looked over at Tristan and sighed. "We were sitting in a nice restaurant only moments ago."

His grin flashed. "I promise I will make it up to you."

She rolled her eyes. "It's hardly a date that you're responsible for."

"Ah, no, you brought it up, so I will absolutely make good on it."

She groaned. "Now you will be obnoxious, won't you?"

He burst into laughter, as she unlocked the door and walked in. "I *will* be obnoxious always," he declared, with a smile. "Now, where would the forensics evidence have gone?"

"Up in the forensics part." She turned to him. "They operate in a different part of this building."

"Good enough." He urged her on with his hand. "Lead the way."

And she did, hoping that somebody would be there. When she walked up to the offices in question, she found several people gathered there. When she stopped in obvious surprise, they looked up and nodded.

"When we're told to put a rush on something," John announced, "we put a rush on it."

"Good to know," she said, as grins flashed in her direction.

"The thing is, you're not the one doing it," John noted.

"No, I'm sure not," she admitted. "I didn't realize we had such a big issue."

"Apparently you picked up a USB key," noted another one of the forensics guys, walking over to her. She thought his name was Tommy. "Are you sure?" he asked, without any accusation or anything malicious in his tone. "We haven't seen any sign of it."

"In which case we've got a problem," Tristan stated, standing at her side. Tommy's gaze narrowed. Tristan nodded. "Yeah, I'm one of the investigators."

"But not one we know," one of the other techs pointed out.

"Maybe not, but you will." Almost an implied threat was inherent in what Tristan said.

Amarylis hurriedly rushed to interrupt the conversation. "Regardless of who knows who, considering I'm new here myself, you need to look for something that looks like a small race car. That's the USB key." They each turned blank looks her way. "Do you remember a small ornamental car?"

"Why would you think that was a key?" asked the fourth member of the forensics team, a woman, walking over to the bags in forensics.

"Because I've seen one before." She waited while the woman went through several bags, and then she caught sight of it herself. "There it is," Amarylis pointed out.

The other woman quickly opened the bag in question and brought out the USB. Everybody gathered around, and they were a bit chaffed. "We wouldn't have initially recognized this as a USB key."

"You would have if you had looked at it close enough," Tristan said. "You can see it here." Pulling it open, the USB connector popped out.

There were several nods. John explained, "Obviously we would have taken a closer look at it later, but it wouldn't have been high on our priority list because it didn't seem to be of too much value or interest."

"I get that," Amarylis noted, "but, because I did find it, I knew what it was. With that knowledge, we need answers as to what's on it."

"Let me go take a look." John took the key over to a computer, and Amarylis sat down nearby, waiting. The three other techs looked at each other and muttered, "I guess maybe we didn't need to come after all."

"You did need to come," stated John, the man at the computer. "If I've got to do extra time, so do you."

"Hey, you're supposed to be nice to the rest of us,"

Tommy joked good-naturedly.

"Did anybody else see anything unique or different at the scene?" Tristan asked, bringing the laughter to a pause.

One by one, his gaze went from one team member to the other, with Amarylis's gaze following along, but everyone shook their heads. "Honestly, these recent crime scenes have been fairly standard for us. Depending on which body you're talking about, we didn't see anything unique or out of order."

"We just didn't notice the key for what it was," Tommy admitted, looking at the miniature car.

"I didn't either," said the female tech from the side, "but we haven't had a chance to process everything, which is where the problem comes in."

She was in no way making an excuse, only an explanation, and that was something that Amarylis herself could understand. Everybody here was so busy and always had so much work to do that it wasn't an unheard-of position to just need time to get through everything. "I understand that," Amarylis agreed. "If I hadn't seen a USB like that one before, we wouldn't be here."

"Good thing you did," John noted. "I'm not exactly sure what we've got here, but it's been encrypted, and I'm just working on getting it unencrypted right now."

Tristan walked over to stand behind him, as the key slowly gave up its secrets. He leaned forward as files began to open. "I'll need copies of everything on this key, and we'll need this whole key backed up and secured."

"Everything here is secure," John noted, looking at him.

"*Extra* secure," Tristan replied.

The technician hesitated, looked over at the coroner, and she nodded.

"We're worried about this going missing, so we'll need multiple backups. Email it to me, email it to him, and you'll need to email it to Jasper, the lead on the investigative team."

"These are names that we don't know," John stated, turning to face Tristan.

Tristan pulled out his phone and contacted Jasper. He looked over at her and added, "You probably need to contact Dr. Cox as well."

She nodded, pulled out her phone. As soon as Dr. Cox answered, she explained the problem.

He said, "Let me talk to them."

She handed her phone over and watched as their faces paled slightly. She winced, as they were given a dressing down as to who and what went to whom. John returned her phone stiffly. Amarylis winced. "I'm sorry. I didn't mean to get anybody in trouble."

"No, that's fine. It's just that we never get told anything."

"I'm sorry about that too. I'm new, and you don't know me all that well yet."

"He's new too." John pointed at Tristan.

"Yes and no, but his department isn't new," she explained. "Definitely some bigger issues are going on here."

"If you say so," John muttered. "As I said, nobody talks to us." The other techs were all quiet, as John followed through on the backups. Then he got up and sealed the key in a processing pouch, labeled it, and put it away in a wall safe for safekeeping.

She smiled and nodded. "Thank you." There weren't too many other comments, and, when Tristan got off the phone with Jasper, Tristan turned and asked, "Any issues?"

"We haven't been reamed out by your boss yet," John

noted stiffly, "but I'm sure that's coming."

"I don't know about being reamed out, but you guys aren't supposed to hand off stuff without a proper chain of command, and, if you don't know who to hand it off to, then that chain of command is compromised. You need to know exactly who and what you're dealing with on each of these cases," he stated, nodding to all of them, "so *that* will change."

Almost immediately several phones went off. They all groaned, but Tristan smiled. "It's still better this way. Your asses are covered, and so are ours."

Multiple phone calls and conversations later, everybody in this group knew exactly who was authorized to work on Mason's case.

When everybody was cleared to go home and to lock up, Amarylis walked back outside with Tristan. "I guess we had to do it that way, *huh*?"

"No, we didn't have to, but you needed to circumvent all the usual red tape," he said, shaking his head. Then he shrugged. "They were doing their jobs by hesitating to give it to us, but we can't tolerate that hesitation from here on out because we need things moving," he shared, with a look in her direction.

"Got it. As long as they don't hold it against me." When he frowned at her. she said, "I know. It doesn't matter."

"It doesn't," he declared. "You are working on a military base now and have more power here than you can possibly imagine. If you want any one of them removed, you can get them removed. They need to follow orders and to realize that *you* are the one giving those orders."

She laughed. "Don't worry. Dr. Cox already gave me that rundown."

"It will just take you a little longer to get your feet wet," he noted, with a gentle smile. As they walked back to his truck, he muttered, "We never did finish that pizza."

"No, we didn't," she agreed and then yawned suddenly.

"Seems time to get you back to your place for bed."

"That sounds good," she replied, "and you can leave me a piece of pizza. I'll make good use of it for breakfast."

He laughed. "Pizza for breakfast, I like it."

"If pizza is good for dinner and lunch, no reason it can't be good for breakfast too."

"I like the way you think." He gave her a big smile. He quickly drove her to her place and got out.

She frowned. "Why are you getting out?"

"Because I will walk you up there to see that everything is as it should be."

She rolled her eyes. "Don't you take the hero thing a bit too far?"

"No, I don't think there's such a thing," he countered, "and, if any trouble comes up, you won't be saying that either."

"No, I wouldn't be." Still, she grumbled the whole way up. As they got up to her apartment, she unlocked the door, stepped inside, and smiled. "See? It's the same as always."

"Good enough. Stay here and be safe and lock up right behind me." And, with that, he handed her the box of pizza.

"Oh, I don't want the whole thing."

"You can have it. I will be working for the next few hours anyway, so I'll get something later." And, with that, he quickly walked out.

She frowned, staring at the large pizza in front of her. "At least take half of it with you."

"No, I'm good." And he was gone.

AS TRISTAN DROVE away, he kept looking in the rearview mirror. Still unsure, he drove around the block a couple times to confirm that nobody had followed him in or out. When he finally got back to the office, Jasper was sitting there. Tristan smiled at him. "You know that Masters or Gideon could show up as needed."

"Masters was here, and I just sent him home."

"Good enough," Tristan replied, as he threw himself into a chair.

Jasper asked, "Did you go through the key?"

"Still looking at it. It's pretty interesting."

"In what way?"

"It seems to be blackmail material."

One eyebrow slowly rising, Jasper asked, "Blackmail of whom?"

Tristan winced. "Appears to be several of our higher-ups, right here on base."

"Okay, that's why the key is so important. Is that also why Drew was killed? Is that why Mason was shot? What's the connection here?"

"Ask me when we get through all this USB data," Tristan replied. "Regardless a lot of the stuff on this key is pretty hot material right now."

Jasper nodded. "Of course, and an awful lot of eyes have seen some of it."

He was worried and should be. "True, but the good stuff is down farther," Tristan murmured. "The USB itself is secured in forensics and will be something that our upper-level brass will need to look at. Damn, if he wasn't in the hospital, that would be Mason's priority, wouldn't it?"

"In this case, I would definitely have thrown it in front of him first," Jasper agreed, "but I won't this time."

They pondered what that would mean in terms of talking to somebody about this blackmail material.

Tristan frowned. "Doesn't sound like a job to look forward to."

"Never is," Jasper muttered, "but we can't exactly ignore this."

"Nope, and, if the blackmail needs to stop, along with the blackmailable activities …"

"We'll likely see a rash of, let's say, *early retirements*," Jasper noted.

At that, Tristan nodded. "So, do we think that Drew was collecting this material, or were the bad buys just getting Drew ready to start blackmailing these people? What was happening here?"

"I don't know," Jasper admitted. "I have somebody coming in right now."

"Somebody we trust?"

Jasper smiled and nodded. "Someone we trust." At that, the door opened, and Mountain strode in.

"Good God, Mountain Bear Rode." Tristan stared up at him. "How the hell do you even fit into uniforms?"

Mountain recognized him right away, and a huge grin flashed across his face. He smacked him hard on the shoulder. "They fit just fine. At least after I get them tailored a little bit."

Tristan got up, gave him a big hug, and asked, "How are you? I heard you had one hell of a time up north."

"Yeah, that I did, but we made it. Teegan, my brother, is recovering, and we're doing well."

"I heard you came home with a lady friend." Tristan was

absolutely amazed and thrilled inside when a flush whispered across Mountain's face.

Then Mountain nodded, with a grin. "Yeah, I lucked out on this one."

"Damn," Tristan muttered. "Hell, if I'd realized that was part of the deal, I might have gone up there myself."

Mountain burst out laughing. "You know how it is, anything to do with Mason. That guy's just got this lovefest going on for the world."

"Yeah, well, right now he doesn't."

"He'll have at again soon enough," Mountain stated comfortably.

"Have you talked to him?"

"Nope, I haven't. I did stop to talk to Tesla though. Mason is doing okay, per the docs, but isn't out of the woods yet. Although there is now eye movement, and he's responding to fingers, hand gestures, so we have some good news, which are all excellent signs of progress."

"I sure as hell hope so," Jasper muttered. "A sniper shooting of Mason is well past the point of being reasonable for anybody."

"Oh, I hear you," Mountain agreed. "Now, what the hell is this about blackmail?"

"Good thing we have you here and now. You have a little experience with blackmail, I hear."

"Yeah, you're not kidding," he muttered. "So come on. Fess up."

At that Jasper got up and walked over to join them. "I would normally be talking to Mason about this."

"Mason is not here, so you talk to me," Mountain stated, with a nod. "Come on. Spill it."

With that, Jasper pointed to Tristan. "He's read more of

the data than I have, to date."

With that preamble, Tristan went into the issues he had just found.

Mountain listened carefully, his jaw clenching and un-clenching, as he quickly processed the information. He nodded and said, "Give me a couple names."

When Tristan mentioned just two, Mountain's eyebrows shot up, and he nodded. "That gives me a direction to avoid then, doesn't it?"

Jasper nodded. "It does, indeed, but the trouble keeps going higher." Jasper wrote down a longer list of names and handed them off to Mountain. Tristan could see most of the names, and several of them made his guts clench. A couple two-star generals were in that mix.

Mountain looked down at the list and groaned. "Yeah, we will have some trouble with this."

"I'm worried that the actual USB might disappear," Jasper shared. "This list of names and alleged activities are all we have to go on for now."

"You have to keep that tight," Mountain confirmed. "Are we thinking that Mason was attacked for this infor-mation?"

"I don't know why Mason would even have had any-thing to do with it," Jasper replied. "That's part of the problem—unless he got wind of it. You know what he's like. He keeps things close, gives somebody a chance, and then that chance blows up."

"But a chance on something like this? Isn't that pushing it, even for him?" Mountain asked.

"Hard to say," Jasper muttered, staring down at the names thoughtfully. "I only see *one* four-star general listed. And one is one too many. So we need to touch base with one who is not compromised."

"Are you on speaking terms with one?" Mountain asked.

"I'm on speaking terms with a *retired* one," Jasper clarified, flashing him a grin, "and he will give us an idea of how to proceed."

"Retired?" Tristan asked. "That won't help."

Mountain shook his head. "I know who Jasper is talking about. This particular one *says* he's retired, but we don't believe it. He's the one who organized that whole operation up north, and he was one who put me and Mason in charge of that op."

"So, he's not op-retired?" Jasper asked.

"These guys are never retired. They just go into black ops." Mountain snorted. "Give me"—he looked at his watch and frowned—"He could still be up. It's not that late."

"No, it isn't, unless you're in your seventies. However, he's a battle ax." Jasper shrugged. "So maybe we should do a conference call."

Mountain quickly pulled out his phone and started texting somebody. When he stopped, he looked over at them and added, "I will keep you guys out of this phone call to begin with, but he'll want to see you."

"Okay," Tristan said, "I'm good with that." Jasper nodded as well.

Mountain asked Jasper, "You are part of Mason's family too, aren't you?"

"Yes, Tesla is my cousin."

"Good, because, at this point in time, we're all more than a little worried about who's invested in Mason's recovery and who wants to see him head to the great beyond."

"We're *all* very invested," Tristan declared.

"Yeah, I hear you. Masters, he's on this team now too, isn't he?" Mountain asked, without looking up from his phone.

"Exactly," Jasper confirmed.

Just then Mountain's phone went off. He saw the number, stood up, and stepped out of the office. They could barely hear him.

"Yes, sir. … No, I need some help on a case." Then the conversation went quiet on Mountain's side. He rejoined them a few minutes later and added, "Now we're in."

"What does that mean exactly?" Tristan asked.

"It means that we have a meeting with him."

"Good, bad, or indifferent?" Tristan asked.

"He's an old warhorse and doesn't believe anything without proof, something I'm very grateful for," Mountain shared. "So, with this blackmail data, he will take it to the next level, as he wants proof of the people involved because a couple of them he's not very happy about."

"What we don't know for sure," Jasper pointed out, "is that the people named in this have done anything wrong."

"No, of course not, and, even if they did, that doesn't mean that they have succumbed to blackmail. It doesn't mean that anybody else knows about whatever it is that they've been getting in trouble with," Mountain explained. "But neither do we know for sure that they haven't done this, so it's got to be handled."

"When you say we have a meeting, when?" Jasper asked.

Mountain smiled at them. "You better tell any partners you have that you won't be home tonight." He glanced down at his watch, and, when a *buzz* came, he nodded. "Let's go."

"Okay, and where are we going?" Tristan asked.

"His house."

Surprised, Tristan followed, and, after an hour's car ride, and then a trip in a helicopter, they landed at a very secure property just outside of a major town. As they descended on the helicopter pad, two men stood there waiting for them. Mountain nodded, as he got out. "Hey, James."

"Interesting times you have here," James replied. "I thought you had more than enough trouble up north."

"I did, but sometimes trouble finds you when you didn't go looking for it."

"Isn't that the truth?" he muttered. "He was just heading to bed."

"He's the one who brought us in, so you and I both know that he calls the shots, and we just all jump."

"No kidding." James laughed. As they proceeded to walk inside the estate, they were led into a small private office. Within seconds of their arrival, the door opened and in walked retired Navy Commander Doran Magellan.

Tristan only recognized him from the news. He stood at attention, but the older man just waved at him. "Relax, son," he barked. "You already brought me a shitload of trouble, so anything you will say to me now," he gave them all a stern stare but landed back on Mountain, "it better be done on a one-to-one basis."

Tristan relaxed at that, then looked over at Mountain, who walked over and gave the older man a gentle hug. "How are you doing?"

"I would be a hell of a lot better if you hadn't brought me this," he grumbled. "If you want to age me, this is the shit that'll do it."

At that, Mountain handed over the paperwork that they had printed off for this meeting. The commander sat down, and, with the three men still standing in front of him, he slowly went from page to page to page. No emotions showed on his face. When he got to the end of the document, he slammed it down and glared at Mountain.

Mountain nodded.

"Damn it, man," the commander muttered, equally quiet. "It's not anything we want to deal with right now. It's not anything I *ever* want to deal with, but here it is." He looked at the other two. "Who have you told?"

"Nobody," Tristan and Jasper replied simultaneously.

"There's that to be thankful for."

"However," Tristan clarified, "this evidence was found on a USB key. Out of an abundance of caution, its contents have been emailed to the four of us, just in case it went missing. Of course the actual key is in evidence at forensics on base."

The commander drummed his fingers on the desk, as he thought about options. He looked over at Mountain, who just nodded. "Oh, I'm glad you came to me about it," the commander admitted, "but damn it. I wish to hell there wasn't anything to come to me about. Why now?"

"That is one of the biggest problems, and we're still investigating in what way this might be connected to the sniper shooting of Mason."

The commander's face sharpened at that comment, as he stared at the men gathered before him. "You do need to figure that out, and fast," he stated. "We can't have any more of this happening. I hear you've got a trail of bodies now as it is." His gaze turned to Tristan. "And you're partly responsible for the bunch of them that showed up yesterday, aren't you?"

Tristan nodded. "Yes, sir."

"It was a good shot, I heard."

"It happened in the hospital, where I was in the ER, getting a head injury checked out. Then we were set upon by the assigned cleaner of the group, so I had to defend myself."

"I don't need the details. If it was a good shot, it was a good shot. And, in the case of these guys"—the commander tapped the blackmail paperwork with two fingers—"I'm not sure I give a damn if it's a good shot or not. I want to ensure this thing goes away forever, and I want to ensure that Mason survives and doesn't get put upon again," he declared. "So bring this to a close, gentlemen."

Jasper nodded. "We are trying, sir."

"Don't try. Just do it," the commander snapped, glaring at him. Then his expression cleared. "You're Jasper."

"Yes, sir," Mountain confirmed. "I did tell you who he was."

The older man just waved his hand. "Yeah, you told me it was Jasper, but you didn't tell me how he was Tesla's cousin."

"I didn't know you knew," Mountain replied.

"Not a whole lot I don't know." He smiled at Jasper. "You do know I'm the godfather to that baby she's carrying."

Jasper grinned. "Yeah, I heard something about that."

"Those two, they're quite the pair—if they could just stay out of trouble, for God's sake."

"I think they were attempting to do that, sir."

"No trials, no more attempts, just get the goddamn job done." He waved at them. "You're dismissed. Go off and do your thing." Lifting the blackmail material, he went on. "*This* is not for anybody else's eyes. I will send men to collect the USB key, and I want all copies, electronic and paper, deleted."

Tristan struggled with that, but he knew it was something he wasn't theoretically allowed to argue with.

Then the commander looked at him and barked, "Speak up."

He hesitated but not for long. "I don't know what you're intending to do with this, sir, but I don't want it to just go under a rock."

The commander asked, "Why not?"

"Because whatever is happening has been going on for a long time. It needs to be cleaned up and cleaned out, not just put away."

Commander Magellan stared at him and then nodded, a slow smile forming. "Takes a lot for somebody to stand up to me," he noted, "but you're right. I have no intention of pushing this under the table, but it does need to be handled discreetly."

"Agreed."

"These men may or may not be involved in something they shouldn't be. They may or may not have done something they shouldn't have," the commander explained. "I won't tar all of them just because we have something here that says they may have gotten involved in something ugly. In one case, I know perfectly well that's not his wife. It's his step-daughter, ... so *that* we'll handle separately as well."

"Right," Tristan replied because he knew well enough not to argue.

"She's also very, very young and has been in his care for a long time. But again, that isn't something that has to go through the courts. We'll talk to the parties and see how we can come up with a solution."

"Maybe it should go to the courts," Tristan ventured.

"If it comes to that, then it will, but it will be *our*

courts," the commander declared, "not the court of public opinion." He stared at Tristan intently and then nodded. "It's good to have morals, son. It's good to have ethics and to stand up for what you believe in. I promise you that I'll make sure that, if these men deserve to be punished or in any way need to be held accountable for a wrongdoing, I will hold them accountable. Is that good enough for you?"

As the commander waited, Tristan thought about it, then nodded. "Yes, sir. Thank you."

"Then we are done here, gentlemen." Looking up at Mountain, he added, "Now I need my beauty sleep. Go."

Mountain laughed. "We'll talk later." And, with that, he led the way back outside again and into the helicopter. Mountain looked over at Tristan with amusement. "I admire you for standing up to him."

Tristan shrugged. "The only thing he can do is fire me."

Mountain laughed. "He admires anybody standing up for anything and everything they believe in. Even if you were wrong, if you believed in it and thought you were right, the commander would appreciate that. What he doesn't like is a yes man. He's had a lifetime of those."

"Can we trust him?" Jasper asked.

Mountain nodded. "Yes, the contents of that file are no longer an issue."

"No longer an issue, except for whoever still wants the contents," Jasper noted.

"That is *your* issue," Mountain noted, with a shrug. "The contents of the file are a completely different story," he clarified. "Now, I have been tasked with the job of picking up the key."

"What about deleting all the emailed copies?"

"Two men are coming, who will be given that job."

Mountain shrugged. Once they landed back at base, he asked, "Which one of you will get me into the forensics lab?"

Jasper looked over at Tristan, who groaned. "I guess I can wake her up again."

"Or you can get Dr. Cox," Jasper offered, with an amused look. "Which is the lesser of the evils?"

Tristan smiled. "I'm always happy to wake up a beautiful woman," he murmured.

Mountain asked. "What? Is this Mason's matchmaking magic at work again?"

"No, no, no," Tristan argued, as he quickly phoned Amarylis. Meanwhile all the guys sat beside him in the vehicle, already on its way to the lab. When she answered, her voice sleepy, Tristan said, "I'm sorry, sweetheart, but we have to get back into the forensics lab."

"When you say *we*," she asked, "who are you talking about?" When he explained, she groaned. "Damn, I was hoping that maybe I would get some sleep one of these days."

"And you will. I promise."

"Yeah, says you. Give me a few minutes to get dressed and to meet you down there."

Tristan looked over at Mountain, who emphatically shook his head. "Apparently we're picking you up," Tristan shared, before she could hang up.

After a moment of silence, she snorted. "*Great.* In that case I guess I'll see you in a few minutes."

"Yes, and not very many of them."

"Got it." She struggled with a yawn. "You know how to show a girl a good time." With that, she ended the call.

Mountain laughed. "Sounds like she's got some spirit."

"She's a new coroner down at the morgue on base," Jasper shared, by way of explanation.

"At least she has more personality than her patients," Mountain muttered.

Tristan laughed at that. "That she does. She is quite the character," he murmured, "but I don't think even she'll be all that tolerant of these midnight trips."

"Maybe not," Jasper pointed out, "but she is the one who found the key."

At that, Mountain looked interested. "You mentioned it was a race car design?"

"Exactly," Tristan replied. "Apparently her father was in sales or something and would hand out novelty items like that. So she instantly recognized what it was."

"Interesting," Mountain murmured. "I can't say that I've seen one quite like that, but I'm not surprised. They come in all shapes and sizes these days."

"Which was her point. When she saw it, she recognized what it was and made sure it got collected, but the forensics team hadn't gotten that far in the lab, and it didn't look like something that would be a priority."

"That's certainly changed now, I presume," Mountain noted.

"It has, but everybody's gone home, and nobody was worried about this case becoming top secret."

"That classification has now changed," Mountain replied, without looking at anybody. When the car pulled up in front of Amarylis's apartment, Tristan got out.

She stood there, her arms crossed, as she tapped her foot impatiently.

He opened the car door and let her inside. "Sorry," he murmured.

She got in and glared at Mountain. "How in the hell do

you even fit into a vehicle like this?"

"Getting in is not so bad," he said. "Getting out is the real bitch."

She stared at him for a moment, then burst into laughter. "Now that I will be happy to see."

CHAPTER 3

WHEN THEY GOT to the coroner's office, even though Amarylis was out of the vehicle first, before she had a chance to head off, Mountain was already out of the car and beside her. The others followed suit.

Mountain grinned at her. "See? Not a problem."

She shook her head. "Your mother must have had a heyday with you."

"Let's just say that disciplining a twelve-year-old already well over six foot tall wasn't an easy thing, but then I didn't do well with discipline at all."

"I can imagine," she muttered. She led the way to the building, quickly unlocked the front door, and led them inside.

"Now," Mountain said, facing her, "I'll need that USB key."

She groaned but headed upstairs to the forensics lab. The door was locked. She frowned as she pointed at it. "I didn't think about that. Who do you want to bring in?" she asked, turning to look at Tristan.

Tristan pulled out his phone and called Dr. Cox. After multiple phone calls back and forth, it took about fifteen minutes before Dr. Cox wandered in, looking tousled and sleepy. He stared at them, as he pulled out his keys. "Do you guys ever go to bed?"

"I keep trying," Amarylis muttered, "but they're not exactly doing anything to promote my beauty sleep."

Tristan laughed. "Good thing you don't need any. You're stunning without it." She rolled her eyes at that, and he rolled his eyes right back. "Honest."

"*Sure*," she muttered, as she looked over to see Mountain grinning at her. She frowned at him. "Glad you think this is funny."

"Not funny at all," he replied, still with humor in his tone. "I might like to get a little bit of sleep in for myself."

"Oh," she muttered. "I guess you all have lives too, don't you?"

"We like to think so," he replied, "but we always seem to have these messes to deal with."

"Isn't that the truth?" She snorted and followed Dr. Cox inside. With him leading the way, they quickly accessed the evidence locker and found the USB key.

Mountain signed for it, and Dr. Cox completed the appropriate documentation to follow military procedures. Then they went to the computers, just as Mountain's phone rang to say that the two men sent to deal with the electronic files had arrived.

By the time they were brought up, Amarylis was fading quickly again, but she knew she wouldn't leave until this circus was over. Whatever was on that USB key was apparently far too important to leave for anyone to access.

By the time the unidentified men were all done with the lab's computers, one turned and addressed Amarylis. "I need access to your emails."

She didn't say a word, just sat down, and logged in.

Then she gave up her seat for one of the two men.

Immediately the men went through and deleted the emails she had just been sent from the lab, and, with that done, the two men did the same thing with Jasper's and Tristan's related emails. When finished, she turned to the two men. "I gather what was on that USB key was something we weren't allowed to see," she murmured.

Those two men didn't respond, but Tristan nodded. "Yes, but it'll be dealt with." She nodded but didn't say anything. He smiled and added, "I promise."

She frowned at Mountain. "It would be a whole lot easier to believe you if it wasn't for all this cloak-and-dagger stuff."

Mountain watched the men finish up with the computer files, then Mountain turned to her. "Cloak-and-dagger is what we do so well." Then he led everybody out of the lab, where they were quickly signed out under the watchful gaze of Dr. Cox, then returned to their vehicles outside.

Mountain walked over to Jasper and pointed. "I will head out right now with these two guys, but I'll talk to you tomorrow." With that, he was gone.

Jasper and Tristan shared a look. "Come on. Amarylis. Time to get you back home again."

"About time," she muttered.

"We're certainly not leaving you here," Tristan said, looking around the dark parking lot. "It surely wouldn't do to leave precious cargo lying around like that."

"That's a good thing." She yawned, too tired to come up with any retort. "I about fell asleep in the lab."

"I doubt it," Tristan countered, with a chuckle. "You were keeping an eye on everything the whole time."

"You bet I was," she grumbled. "Worst case scenario, I

get my ass kicked for letting that information go."

"No, a whole lot of people with a much higher rank than you have right now are totally involved with the USB key," Jasper shared, with a smile in her direction. "So, in this case, you are free and clear."

"Maybe," she muttered, uncertain. "Still doesn't change the fact that a lot of people have died, quite possibly for that USB information. I want to make sure that nobody else does." As she was dropped off at her place, she looked up and groaned.

"Problem?" Tristan asked, as he got out beside her.

She shook her head. "Just hoping for more hours to be left in the night."

"Right, and you've got a full day coming up."

"Yes, and no way I can call in sick," she noted, with an irritable expression, "so thanks for that."

He gave her a gentle smile. "Hey, welcome to my world."

She nodded, as she looked over at him. "It can't be that easy."

"Some days it's easy, and some days it's not," he replied, with a nod. "We come up against wonderful new cases all the time. This is just another one."

"Good enough." She sighed, as she walked to her apartment. He followed her. "What? You're not walking me back up again, are you?"

"I wasn't at first, but then I decided I would." He quickly raced up the stairs with her. As they got to her apartment, he walked in, walked through the place, checked it out, looked under the bed, into her closets, then came back to the front door.

She stood there, with her arms crossed over her chest.

"Was that necessary?"

"Maybe not, but it'll make me feel better." With that, he leaned over and gave her a quick kiss on her cheek. "Now you can get some sleep." And then he was gone.

She stared at his back as he left, her fingers on her cheek, as she wondered what the hell had just happened to her nice orderly world, because somehow someone had just blown it all apart, and she had no idea how the pieces would ever fit back together again.

TRISTAN WOKE THE next morning, stretched, and rolled over, wishing he could grab another six hours, but something prodded at him. He opened his eyes and heard his phone buzzing. He snatched it up and saw the ID as *Jasper*. "Problems?" he barked into the phone.

Jasper snorted. "Isn't there always?"

"Sure, but do you have something specific?"

"No, everything's holding at the moment."

"I'm glad to hear it. So what's this call about?"

"Yeah, we have a meeting first thing at nine."

"Great, and will we get raked over the coals?"

"Doesn't matter if we are or not," Jasper stated. "We're just giving our names and the names of those who put us in this position."

"*Great*, because, according to all these upper-level brass, we are nobodies."

Jasper chuckled. "Just never let them hear you say that."

"Got it."

As Tristan headed for the shower, he wondered just what the day would bring. He was pretty sure that, once they were cleared from their midnight activities—assuming they got cleared—it would be right back onto the trail as to what was happening with Mason's case.

The fact that they hadn't connected this blackmail scheme to the mastermind trying to take out Mason was a bigger concern. Yet there had to be a connection—although, so far, it just led to the hired help, now all dead. The USB key was found at the crime scene for the real Drew's death, Drew the sniper. Plus the woman who had posed as Drew's sister and who had knocked out Tristan, sending him to the hospital, she was now dead. That woman may have been the girlfriend to the squatter watching Drew's house from Pearl's house, killed by Gideon in self-defense. They also had a dead cleaner, the fixer, whom Tristan had killed in self-defense in the hospital, recognizing the hitman as the professional cleaner hired to scrub away the blood in Pearl's house. Tristan figured that the fixer had killed the others so far.

None of this made Tristan feel any better about their progress. They were getting deeper into this hole, not clearer, and that's exactly what they were told as soon as they got to the meeting. Their boss was not impressed about the midnight activities either.

"You know perfectly well you should have come to me," he snarled.

Jasper didn't say anything; he just waited.

"How the hell would that old bat of a commander have anything to do with this? And why should he?"

"Commander Magellan?" Tristan murmured, and Jasper nodded.

Their immediate boss rambled on. "He phoned me *early* this morning, waking me up to tell me what happened, stating that you guys are to be completely cleared of all wrongdoing. That's not for him to tell me."

Tristan waited while their boss ranted and raved about people with power trips who should have retired ages ago. Tristan understood the sentiment, and he understood perfectly well not being happy when somebody stepped on your toes. However, Tristan and Jasper had no choice, at least not much, not once Mountain had been brought into the matter. Sure enough, once Mountain had been brought in, things had moved very, very quickly, just not necessarily the way their immediate bosses would have wanted.

When they were finally dismissed, walking to the investigation department, Tristan looked over to see Jasper smiling. "What's so funny? You may have enjoyed having him chew us up and spit us out, but, damn, I sure didn't."

Jasper just laughed. "It's always about power, you know? Who's got the power to step on the toes of someone else. In this case, our boss didn't have the power to even be informed about it, and that's what he's upset about."

"He has every right to be upset. I sure would be," Tristan said.

"I get it," Jasper replied, "yet it's well past our authority."

"That was made pretty clear last night." Tristan smirked. "Mountain can sure make things happen. Not only is he a mountain in sheer size but he moves mountains. You've got to love and trust and appreciate having him in our corner."

"He had one hell of a time a while back, when his brother went missing up north. That was a convoluted mess, but he kept at it, and finally they found him and eventually brought him home safe. The best thing, after finding his brother, was that Mountain showed up to lead the search and rescue, and now he's hooked up with a female doctor and researcher. Amelia Morrison is her name. He deserves to be happy, but he sure got us into the soup last night, though he's probably laughing about the whole thing. It seems like we spend a good share of our time in hot water these days."

"Maybe, but it still sucks."

"Don't worry about it, Tristan. You aren't in trouble. I'm not in trouble, and honestly, neither is our boss, by doing it the way we did it. It was taken completely away from him too, so he's not in trouble either, something he'll realize fairly quickly."

"If you say so," Tristan muttered, "but it won't be today."

"No, it won't be today and probably won't be tomorrow. It may not even be the day after that." Jasper grinned. "Still, he'll come to understand fairly quickly."

"Now we need to track everything surrounding the movements of the people in the morgue," Tristan suggested, "to confirm that we know exactly where each of our dead foot soldiers were in the last what? Four days? Or maybe even before Mason got shot. We've got the bodies, so all we need to do is track them and connect them to each other."

"Whoever hired the sniper, Drew, may or may not have had anything to do with that information on the USB key, but somebody in that group of the recently dead must be connected to the blackmailer or one of the blackmailees, as a lot of names were on the USB. We have the names of the dead too, but we probably need pseudonyms for them as well, to see if they connect to any of our names on the blackmail list."

Tristan nodded. "I agree."

Jasper continued. "I think somebody from that blackmail group must be connected to Mason, and somebody from Mason's life is connected to this blackmail group. At some point they decided that Mason was responsible for their secrets getting out, so they hired the sniper. Then they went in and cleaned up all the threads linking the mastermind with the hired guns."

"Interesting theory, and it makes sense."

"It absolutely does," Jasper confirmed. "The trouble is, we're not allowed to know about those blackmail names, and nobody else is allowed to know either. I did glance at the email when it was sent to me, but I didn't get very far into it. Considering the fact that we already do know several higher-ups who were on that list, we will give each of them a number, not a name but a number, and we will work up a chart. Do you remember very much of what was on those USB files?"

Tristan smiled. "Photographic memory, or at least close to it."

"Awesome." Jasper rubbed his hands together in excitement. "We just need to assign each person ID'd on that USB with a number and their corresponding blackmail activity—affairs, theft, treason, whatever it is." Jasper opened the door to their offices and headed inside. Tristan followed.

"I can do that," Tristan replied, as he grabbed a chart board. "I suggest we use the first letter of their first names, and correlate that to their assigned numbers, and then we will add more names if need be right after that. You just sort it out, and tell me what it is you want." And, with that, Tristan set up the big chart board with the first five names from the USB, using a numerical system, and then he wrote down a simple letter to start the word of whatever their blackmail activity was. Only one he wasn't sure about.

When he turned and looked at Jasper, he pointed to the

chart. "Take a look at this. It's the activity of the last one that I'm not sure about."

"You've got the gay affair, the selling arms, and … right, the trafficking. I'm not sure what that other two are all about."

"I'm not exactly sure either, but I think this one was pay-to-play, giving promotions and demotions for money," he suggested, with a snort.

"Wow, that's pretty shitty, and what's this last one?"

"That's the one I'm not sure about."

Jasper looked over at him, his tone grim when Tristan confirmed this as buried in the USB files. "*That*'s the one?"

"Yeah, at the end of the key."

"I remember it clear as a day. That's treason."

CHAPTER 4

AMARYLIS WOKE UP the next morning, a bit achy and sore. It took her a moment to remember the events of the night before, including the trip to the morgue, outside of office hours. She was quiet for a moment, just thinking about the implications, then slowly got up, had a shower, and drove to work.

As she walked in, Dr. Cox called out to her. She headed to him, one eyebrow raised. "Problems?"

He snorted. "Not so much problems, but I've told the lab staff a little bit about last night.'

"Ah, I'm sure that didn't make people too happy."

"Nope, it sure didn't." Cox smiled. "I've also heard from various bosses this morning that there is to be no discussion about it. It has to be kept totally under wraps, so you need to be extra careful around people. No mentioning, no questions, no nothing."

"Got it," she said. "I wasn't planning on it."

"Just a reminder."

At that, the conversation turned to work, and she headed to her office to take care of a bunch of reports, before starting on the day's autopsies. As she sat down, her phone buzzed. She looked over to see it was Tristan. She smiled as she answered it. "And here I thought you won't be letting me out of your sight," she teased.

"I followed you to work," he shared. "I'm not there with you, though that depends if you're safely locked up inside."

She stared down at the phone. "You followed me in?"

"I did," he confirmed, with a cheerful tone that grated on her nerves a bit. "I was trying to get there before you left, so I could talk to you, but I didn't let you know I was on my way. When I saw you coming out of your apartment, I just ensured you got to work safely."

"You could have stopped and talked to me at work," she stated. "You don't have to do all this cloak-and-dagger stuff."

"I hope I don't have to. If I did, I've already failed because I should have been at your place overnight."

"You certainly don't need to do that," she stated.

"Again I hope not, but we don't know anything yet to assuage my fears."

"Right, I was hoping you might have some updates."

"I would love to have some updates." He chuckled. "However, because of the USB key you found, we have a lot more leads to follow."

"Probably a good thing," she agreed. "I still can't believe last night happened. Can you?"

"You have no idea. I can't even tell you how the rest of my night went, plus my morning so far, but I barely got any sleep."

"Sorry about that. You could have come into my office and got coffee here."

He laughed. "I know, but I'm already heading back to my office."

"You still need to look after yourself," she scolded.

"I will, and does missing out on coffee at your place

mean I'm not looking after myself?"

Such a curious tone filled his words that she had to laugh. "It's probably totally fine for you to just do whatever you're used to doing," she acknowledged, "because I'm sure you're well used to doing exactly what you want."

"Ooh, I don't know about that," he replied, with a chuckle, "but, if you're going anywhere today, I do need to know, so I can come over there to follow you."

"I might be traveling with my job," she shared, "but that shouldn't affect you."

"Yet it does. We don't know who is after that USB key, who might think that *you* still have it. Plus, if anybody saw us remove it, that'll be the next challenge. Either way, it involves you."

"You think somebody could be after me over it?" she asked in astonishment. "I figured now that it was gone that it would be a nonissue."

"I hate to point this out, but how will the bad guys know it's gone?"

She wrinkled up her nose at that thought. "*Great.* Something else I was hoping to not put together."

"Exactly. Anyway I would suggest lunch."

"Lunch would be nice," she said, and then she frowned. "Or is this just about work?"

"Nope, it's not just about work. How about twelve, and I'll pick you up outside." And, with that, he disconnected.

She stared down at the phone, shaking her head. She wasn't sure that she got a clearcut answer as to whether this lunch was work or whether it was something else. The thought that it might be something else worried her, yet put a smile on her face.

Something was very engaging about Tristan, also heartwarming, when a man took it upon himself to ensure you were safe—not that she'd ever had too many issues with being *not* safe. Still, with whatever was going on here at base, she definitely felt a degree of comfort in knowing Tristan was around.

Dr. Cox poked his head in her office at that moment, and his eyebrows shot up. "Now what put that look on your face?"

She flushed. "I don't know what you're talking about."

He laughed and teased, "If that were the case, you wouldn't be blushing. The fact that you are makes my heart swell with joy. This old man has always been a romantic at heart."

She groaned and rolled her eyes at him. "If that's the case, how come you live alone?"

His smile fell off. "I lost my wife of thirty-four years some six months ago." He then took a moment to add, "And I'm not quite ready to move on from that."

She winced. "Oh, God, I'm so sorry."

"Don't be." He gave a wave of his hand. "You couldn't have known, and it just means you've not been gossiping about me, and I appreciate that. Now I need some help, so get your butt in here."

And, with that, the focus of her day returned to work.

TRISTAN ENDED THE call, tossed his cell on the seat beside him, and turned to look at the coroner's building in front of him. He didn't want her to know that he was here, keeping an eye on the place. Yet, after talking to Jasper, it had been determined that somebody needed to keep an eye out to confirm nobody would get in to retrieve that USB key.

It was all fine and dandy, until something went wrong, and Tristan couldn't afford for anything to go wrong. They were working on getting more men to help, and—until that happened, and he was relieved from his current post—he would sit here in the morgue's parking lot because a mistake now could be a permanent mistake that nobody wanted to see happen.

He watched several vehicles come and go, and then noted that one of the vehicles had pulled up along with several others, yet the driver remained inside it. Tristan frowned at that as he watched the guy, but the driver just sat there, studying the building. From his position, Tristan was largely hidden from everybody else's view, a position he'd taken deliberately, but it also gave him a bird's eye view of this new arrival.

He quickly marked down everything he could see about the vehicle. As he wondered if he should walk past to get an ID on the driver's face, the car door opened, and the driver stepped out.

The tall streak of a male stood up, dressed in a jeans jacket over jeans and a white T-shirt. He looked typical of almost everybody else on base who was off duty, as he walked toward the building. He looked around casually, but something was almost professional about that expression on his face. It was enough to set Tristan's mood on edge, as this was exactly what he had been sitting here waiting for.

He quickly sent a text message to Jasper and one to Amarylis. Then Tristan hopped out of his vehicle and walked up at a faster pace, reaching the glass double entrance doors at almost the same time as the other guy. Smiling at him, Tristan said, "Hey, haven't seen you around here before."

The other guy just nodded. "Not exactly a place I frequent."

"Right, not a place most people want to even visit," Tristan replied in a joking tone.

The other guy just stared at him and continued inside. As Tristan reached the second set of double doors, these all wood with no windows, the other guy lagged behind, either as if unsure where he was going or waiting to see what Tristan would do. Choosing the option of going through the double doors, Tristan completely ignored the other guy and soon sat down on the nearby stairs, making it look like he was taking a phone call.

He couldn't see what the other guy was doing through the solid wood doors. He waited a moment, and then the doors opened, and the guy stepped in, looking up at him. But Tristan was talking on the phone—or making it look like that way. The other guy glanced at him, then looked down and proceeded to go up the stairs.

Ignoring him, Tristan continued with his fake phone call. When the other guy disappeared onto the second floor's landing, Tristan stood and raced up behind him. However, he saw no sign of him as he got to the second floor. Still, this worried Tristan, as this guy had reached the floor where the evidence in the lab was held. It wouldn't have taken a whole lot to figure out where that was. Yet it was also more confirmation of where this guy was headed.

As Tristan walked down the hall to the lab, his phone buzzed. Amarylis had sent him a text, with a series of question marks and **WTF?** He smiled at the expression because she wasn't saying anything, yet said everything. As he walked to the lab, he headed directly in, whereas the other guy loitered outside, as if checking his messages.

Tristan stepped inside the lab to see several of the forensics guys glaring at him. "Glare all you want," he declared, with a nod.

"You took evidence out of here."

"Me? God, no. Yet one of your higher-up bosses did that, and you might want to keep that in mind."

"You know that isn't common procedure," John said stiffly.

"Then take it up with your direct boss," Tristan suggested, with cheer in his tone. "In the meantime, we have a problem."

John groaned. "Now what?"

"I think a guy just outside may be looking for the item in question, and what you need to do is keep your mouth shut in the event that he asks."

"We know nothing about it," John stated stiffly, "and we do know how to do our jobs, … even if other people keep screwing us over."

"Anytime you want to make a formal complaint, take it up with the brass. For the record, it doesn't matter what I would have done. It was way over my head too."

They had to acknowledge that because, when it came down to the brass placing orders, Tristan wouldn't put his own neck on the line for these tech guys. Yet, if they had any sour grapes about it, which he would if he were them, they needed to take it up the line. "I presume you already talked to Dr. Cox about it?"

"Yeah, and we were told it's been dealt with."

"I'm sure it has," Tristan replied, knowing that, if not for the trust he had in Mountain, no way in hell Tristan would be happy with the scenario either.

When the door opened, Tristan turned to see the new

arrival studying the lab area. One of the lab techs walked over to the front counter and in a cold voice stated, "I think maybe you're lost."

The other man shook his head. "No, I don't think so. I'm looking for the lab."

"You found the lab, but this isn't open to the public."

"Maybe it should be," he declared, with a sneer.

The other guy stiffened and stared at him. "What the hell?"

"Yeah, what the hell?" he repeated. "I came here for something specific, and I'm not exactly seeing what I want."

"What is it you want?" he asked.

"I want the damn USB key that was turned in," he stated, and suddenly a black snub-nosed gun appeared in his hand.

The techs gathered nearby stared at the gunman in shock, then all turned to Tristan. He stepped up and said, "Whoa, whoa, whoa. What the hell is this?"

"Exactly what I said it was. I want that key."

Tristan shook his head. "Not something we can give you."

"Doesn't matter if you can give it to me or not," he snapped, his cold smile letting Tristan know he didn't give a shit who or how.

"You do realize you're on camera, right?" Tristan asked.

The gunman shrugged. "By the time the yahoos around here sort it all out, I'll be long gone, and it's not your problem. Your problem is getting me the key."

"If we're talking about evidence that was taken from a crime scene recently," Tristan noted cheerfully, "we don't have it."

"If you don't have it, I don't see any reason to keep you

alive." Hearing the gasp behind him, Tristan narrowed his gaze on the man in front of him. "That's interesting. You've come here to murder people? It doesn't matter who, when, or how? If we don't have what you want, we're dead, is that it?"

As the handgun raised, Tristan stilled himself, yet his right hand was holding his own revolver in his jacket pocket, pointed right at the stranger. He would shoot if needed, but, at this point, he would rather not because he needed more information than what he currently had. So he must keep the gunman talking, if he could. "So, let me get this straight. Something was found at a crime scene, which you obviously don't want anybody to know about it. So you came here in broad daylight, in full sight of the cameras, to a *military* building, to steal it from us, using a whole lot of threats and a gun for a little persuasion?"

"I would have thought that was pretty evident," the man said in a bored tone of voice, as he looked from one to the other. "Who's the boss here?"

When they pointed at Tristan, he sighed. "Nice to know we're thrown to the wolves so easily. Thanks, guys. Thanks for throwing me under the bus." Yet he didn't blame these guys in the least. This was not what they were cut out for, and they knew he was part of the investigative team. Therefore, by pointing him out, they trusted him to handle it. Yet it wouldn't make this any easier.

The gunman smiled. "I guess you're the lucky one then, aren't you?"

"Maybe so," Tristan replied. "Still doesn't change the fact that what you're after isn't here."

The gunman shrugged his shoulders. "I don't want to listen to anything you have to say, but I do want to see that key."

One of the forensics guys walked over with a little bag and inside was a plain USB key.

The guy's face lit up. "See? This is what happens when you have the proper motivation," he noted, snarling at Tristan.

Tristan nodded. "You know that this is a bad idea though, don't you?"

"It doesn't matter," he declared.

For the first time, Tristan saw a note of almost desperation in the stranger's hard gaze, as he waved his gun.

"Sometimes, when you're backed up against a wall, you've just got to do it."

"Sometimes doing it is what backs you up against the wall," Tristan explained, his tone equally hard.

The gunman glared at him. "Save your preaching for somebody who gives a shit."

Tristan didn't say anything, just waited until the gunman looked at them individually, as if assessing what his next move would be. Tristan waited, equally still.

The man shifted nervously, leaving Tristan to wonder whether he would take off or check the key for the material he was after, though something about his attitude suggested he probably had no clue what was on it.

"I hope it's worth it," Tristan added.

The gunman glared at him, then looked around again, as he slowly backed up to the door. "Of course it is." With that, he was gone.

Tristan raced to the door, turning to look at the techs, still standing there, staring at him. He pulled out his phone and called Jasper. "He's coming outside right now," he snapped.

"I've got two men near the door," he muttered, "and I'm just coming into the parking lot myself."

"He's been given a key, but it's not the right one."

"Good thinking, but also bad thinking because, if he gets away, he'll be back."

"I doubt *he* will come back. Just by doing what he's done, this guy has pulled his own trigger."

"Not your problem. Remember that."

He turned and glanced back at the techs, still staring at him. "Stay here." And, with that, he ducked out after the gunman. He raced all the way down the stairs, and, when he got to the bottom, the gunman stood at the double glass doors, staring at the two MPs outside.

He turned to Tristan and glared. "You know this won't go well."

"It won't go well for you either," Tristan replied. "If you go outside, they will take you down."

"Not if you are my prisoner," the stranger suggested, with a laugh, pointing the handgun at Tristan.

"I'm not talking about those two MPs. I'm talking about whomever conned you into doing this. Do you think they will let you survive this?"

"What are you talking about?"

"Everybody involved in this mess has been taken out, shot dead, even when they weren't expecting it."

"Seeing as how I was forced to do this, I highly doubt it."

"I suppose you were told to walk outside and to show them the USB key in your hand."

The gunman nodded. "Yep, that's how they'll know I got it, and thank God I did. Are you prepared to take a bullet?"

Tristan sighed. "Not at all. I never intended to take a bullet. However, if you go out there, you will get your ass kicked in a permanent way."

The gunman shook his head. "No, you don't understand. They need this, and it's my job to get it."

"Why? What have they got on you?"

"Doesn't matter what they've got on me," he snapped, his voice loud, angry, and a little bit hysterical.

Tristan winced. "Is there anything I can say to keep you from going out there?"

"No, there isn't. One way or another, this is what I've got to do."

"You don't have to though. You could choose another path."

He snorted. "What are you, some holier-than-thou preacher?"

"No, man, not at all. Just somebody who knows what's in your future, the minute you go out that door."

He shook his head. "Even with your two MPs out here, it doesn't matter. I've got people watching out for me. They will shoot down those MPs." When his phone buzzed, he nodded. "That's my signal that it's clear to go." He pushed open the door and stepped outside.

A moment of hesitation followed, even while Tristan remained inside, looking for the most likely spot where the bad guys' sniper was at. Meanwhile, the two MPs outside stepped up closer to the gunman.

The gunman held up the key for all to see. "Gentlemen, I'm taking this, and you can do whatever the hell you want, but I'm walking out of here."

A single shot sounded clearly, and Tristan followed the trajectory and pushed open the double doors, motioning the two MPs after the sniper. Then Tristan walked over to the fallen gunman's body. A single bullet hole was right between his eyes.

He looked over at Jasper, who joined him now to ask, "What the hell was that all about?"

Tristan quickly explained that the gunman was supposed to hold up the USB key.

"The key is very distinctive, isn't it?" Jasper asked.

"It is, so obviously he didn't have the right key," Tristan stated. "I didn't tell him that he had the right key, but I did try to convince him not to come out here. He said he had to. So I presume he was being blackmailed along with the other names on our list. He mentioned that he needed to do this, so that's most likely about blackmail."

"Maybe." Jasper looked down at the body. "But, man, he's paying a heavy price for keeping whatever it is a secret."

"And not only that, it will no longer be a secret," Tristan declared, facing Jasper. "We will tear apart his life."

CHAPTER 5

AMARYLIS WAS JUST cleaning up, taking off her apron and her gloves, when Dr. Cox walked over and asked to see her for a moment. "Problems?"

As she walked over to her office, he stepped inside, closed the door, and quickly gave her a story she had a hard time believing. "He walked into the lab with a gun?" she asked in shock.

He nodded.

"What about the security guard?"

"He was not at his post."

She stared at him and shook her head. "But that means ..." Then she fell silent.

"Yes. That's exactly what that means."

She shook her head again. "So, now what?"

"Now, not to mention the fact that we have a body to process out in front of the building, there will also be an investigation as to how he got the gun through our supposed security."

"Of course." She pinched the bridge of her nose. "And I thought Tristan was overreacting."

"What do you mean? Have you talked to him today?"

She quickly filled him in on the text she got.

"So, he's been sitting out in the parking lot?"

She nodded. "Yes, he suspected somebody was coming after the key."

"Obviously they decided that doing it secretively wouldn't work."

"Surely these bad guys had to expect some repercussions."

"I think the trick here was that the bad guys were looking to see if we had the key or not. When one of the lab techs gave our gunman a dummy key, he took it and ran. When he went outside and held it up, as directed, the bad guys would have known it was the wrong one."

She nodded. "The little car design is fairly distinctive. So now they will be wondering whether it's here or whether somebody tried to cheat the gunman. Yet we have no way to know because he's dead." She walked over and grabbed her medical bag. "Is this body for you or me?"

"I suggest we both go take a look, and we will need the forensics guys too."

She winced at that. "They won't be too impressed if they were already dealing with him, as the live gunman in their faces."

"I don't think anybody is too impressed at the moment, but we will all do our jobs because we're professionals."

She walked out the front doors with him to see a small crowd had gathered. Tristan detached himself and walked over to join them with a smile. "Are you okay?"

"I don't know. You keep giving me work."

A grin flashed across his face. "In that case, I will say you're doing okay." He looked over at Dr. Cox. "And you?"

Dr. Cox nodded. "But you know as well as I do, young man, that we need this to stop," he noted bitterly. "It's one thing to have this happening out in the world, but another thing entirely when my own office is targeted."

"Got it," he murmured. "I did talk to the gunman, and he did appear to be pressured to do this. I tried to convince him to *not* go outside and to *not* hold up the key, but he wasn't listening to reason."

"And, of course, you knew it was the wrong USB key."

He nodded at that. "Are you bringing your forensics techs down here now?"

"We've got the three who were up there, but I've asked them to stand by, to remain in the lab," Dr. Cox explained. "I've got another team coming in to give us a hand with the crime scene itself."

"I can only imagine the work involved in your morgue this week."

"Yeah. At this point, my own damn lab needs to be analyzed as a crime scene."

"It was a pretty clear-cut shooting," Tristan shared, "and we weren't the shooters."

"That's a good thing," Dr. Cox muttered. He stopped in front of the body, then looked around and shook his head. "He didn't even get off the front step."

"His orders were to hold up the key and to show them that he had it. He probably thought there would be cover fire to give him a way to get out from under our two MPs and to ensure he got away. So much for that thought. What about your security system here?"

"That's an interesting question. How did he even get inside with a gun?" Dr. Cox asked.

"And, for that matter, how did I?" Tristan asked.

"You had a gun too?" Amarylis asked, staring at him.

He nodded. "By the time he walked in, I had mine in

my jacket pocket, so I could shoot if I needed to."

"Jeez," she muttered, "so our security guard was out of pocket and our scanners aren't working either."

"The guard was told that someone else took his shift today. We'll check more into that. As for your scanners, I think they've been turned off."

Dr. Cox closed his eyes, his face red and heading to purple. "That is something I will deal with right now." He looked at Amarylis and asked, "Are you okay to process this?"

She nodded and walked over to the gunman. Somebody had thrown a blanket over his face. She pulled it back, took one look, and sighed.

"Do you recognize him?" Tristan asked.

"No, I sure don't. I've never seen him before in my life."

As she worked, she noted that Tristan was staying close but off to the side. When she finally managed to stand up and to step away, leaving the forensics team to process the scene, she looked over at Tristan. "You don't think it's over, do you?"

"They didn't get the key, did they?"

She winced and nodded. "Do you think giving him the fake key was the wrong thing for these guys to do?"

"No. From their point of view, it got the gunman off their backs in that moment. I can't blame them for that. They're all just hoping to go home at the end of the day and to not have to deal with this. Plus, they probably couldn't have fathomed what to me was a given."

"So, you're assuming the bad guys will return."

"Yes. They feel they need the USB key, and, considering the information that's on it, I doubt that they will give up quite so easily."

She frowned and nodded. "Do you think the blackmail-ees did anything to get themselves killed?"

"I don't know. I don't know the situation these guys are in, but this one today definitely showed signs of desperation."

"He told you that he was under pressure to do this?" she asked.

Tristan nodded. "I assumed at the time that it was blackmail related, but I didn't get a chance to confirm it with him. He went outside with the key in his hand, unconcerned with the two MPs Jasper had stationed out here. So, as ordered, our gunman held up the key as soon as he was outside and took a bullet between the eyes."

"Jeez," she muttered. "Then again the stuff that's on that key must be pretty damning."

"It's very damning. What the bad guys don't know is that it's already too late, and we have it."

"Or had it," she corrected, turning to face him.

"*Had it* is right," he confirmed, with a frown.

"So, do you trust the guys who ended up with the key?"

"I trust the person I was dealing directly with, yes," he clarified. "I can understand the doubt on your part, but Mountain is as trustworthy as they come, and he's got connections."

She shrugged. "As long as you're sure, it doesn't matter to me," she muttered. "Yet right now, all of it seems suspect."

"That's because some pretty big names are involved in that blackmail list, some with pretty big positions, and nobody will be very happy if any of this information gets loose, particularly if it goes to a foreign body."

"Ouch, I hadn't considered that potential, but I guess,

once a person's integrity is compromised to that degree, the stakes just get even higher."

"Sure does," Tristan agreed, with a nod. He looked around and asked, "How much more do you have to do here?"

"Not a whole lot more to do," she replied. "Just this one scene. We'll track his pathway up the stairs and into the lab and then back outside again, but I highly doubt we will find anything else. We have witnesses. You and the rest of the techs," she noted. "So, once we've got questions asked and answered, we'll be done, though I'm quite concerned about the staff."

"We should be concerned. Jasper's talking about getting some additional guards in here."

"And yet will that make a difference?"

"The fact that today's guy came in with a weapon is a problem, and I'm still not exactly sure how he did that. When I saw that he came straight in, I brought my weapon right in too."

She smiled. "I guess we can be grateful for that. At least you didn't have to use it this time."

"No, I didn't, but the minute I knew he was determined to come outside, it was already a lost cause for him."

"How pathetic and sad is that?" she said, shaking her head. "Obviously somebody's pretty desperate."

"Desperate people make mistakes," Tristan noted, then hesitated.

She eyed him and asked, "What?"

"Just wondered if you picked up on the fact that he was taken out by a sniper?"

She winced. "I hadn't made that connection, but thanks for that reminder. So, are we thinking this is connected to your friend in the hospital?"

"Oh, I'm pretty sure it somehow connects to Mason," Tristan replied, as he watched the techs work. "We haven't been able to find out how yet."

"And that's the worst, isn't it? You know that there's a problem, and you're trying your best to make sure that problem is dealt with. Yet, every time you turn around, there's a new player."

"The only player that I'm interested in at this point is the one who pulled the trigger today. This guy here was just a patsy and didn't need to die. If he'd listened to me, we might have had a chance at keeping him alive," Tristan explained.

"Why is that?"

"He was more than determined to keep his own secret under wraps, but now? Now I just get to rip apart his life and find it out anyway." And, with that, he grimaced at her.

She wondered what was on his mind. "I would say lunch or coffee is out for the moment."

He half smiled, apparently amused at the absurdity of the situation. "That was my take too. I need to head back to the office to see what I can find on this guy."

"If you find anything of interest, please let me know," she said. "We'll do our job here, but, if you've got anything to offer or to add, it would sure be a help."

"I hear you. I'll share whatever I find." And, with that, he turned and walked away.

TRISTAN WALKED INTO the investigative department to find Jasper standing there, with both Morgan and Sam glaring at him. Tristan raised an eyebrow. "Obviously things here are a little tense, so am I in the way or am I in the middle of it?" he asked.

"You're right in the middle of it," Sam snapped.

"Look. We don't get in the middle of these kinds of things," Morgan said in a somewhat calmer tone.

"That's nice," Tristan replied cheerfully. "So what do you expect me to do when a gunman stands there in the lab, pointing his weapon around?" he asked, tilting his head, staring at Morgan, still wearing a smile on his face. "Am I supposed to walk away, leave those lab guys to twist in the wind because it's *not my job?*"

Morgan held out his hands. "All I'm saying is that we don't get involved in these kinds of things."

"What do you mean, *we don't get involved in these kinds of things?*" Tristan asked in disgust. "That just makes me suspicious as hell as to what you *do* get involved in," he snapped, as he looked over at Sam.

Sam's eyebrows shot straight up, and he shook his head. "I sure as hell hope you aren't suggesting anything irregular is coming out of this office,"

"*Irregular* has been the *only thing* that defines this office since Jasper arrived." Tristan crossed his arms, leaned back against the door jamb, and stared at them. "I still fail to see what you guys do while you're here."

"What are you talking about? We work our asses off." Morgan had lost his cool now too.

"And yet you *accomplish* nothing." That came from the boss who had walked up behind them.

"That's not true," Sam declared, his face turning motley red. "You're the one who stopped us from working on one of the cases."

The boss just glared at him and turned to look at Morgan. "Morgan, what do you have to say about this?"

Morgan shook his head. "We're just figuring out what's going on right now," he said, raising both hands. "Apparently having Tristan here involved in some confrontation was okayed by Jasper. Not only that, but they also removed some evidence from the lab, and that will never go over well."

Jasper gave Morgan a hard smile. "In that case, call retired Commander Magellan and complain to him yourself."

Sam stared at him in shock. "What?"

"You heard me," Jasper continued, then looked from Sam to Morgan and back to his immediate boss. "You can call him too, if that's what you all need to get over it."

"I already have," the local boss snapped, then looked to Sam and Morgan, who were clearly still shell-shocked by the name drop. "That shit happens," the boss declared, "and they've pulled the information."

"That's not allowed," Sam argued, snarling. "We don't have people in this world that just get to pull something collected as evidence."

Tristan frowned, as Sam seemed to have completely forgotten that his own boss had stopped his investigation into the disappearance of their own investigator, Nicholas.

Yet, when that boss turned to glare back at Sam, it was obvious that the boss hadn't forgotten.

"Oh," Morgan muttered, turning to face his boss. "Is that why you had us stop the investigation into Nicholas?"

"There are things you don't need to know about," the boss declared stiffly, "but questioning me definitely won't get you any answers."

"Maybe not," Sam spat, turning to look at him. "Yet how do we know that we haven't accidentally been involved in some of this bloody bullshit ourselves, just by following orders?"

"You don't," the boss declared, staring at him. "Get used to it. That's the way the military works."

"Not always," Sam argued. "This is supposed to be the job we do, investigating the people who do this shit. We're not supposed to be the ones doing it."

"Doing what?" the boss asked, his tone turning hard and cold. "Remember who you're talking to."

Sam shook his head. "I don't have to remember who I'm talking to. I'm talking to the man who had us stop working on the case of our own missing investigator." He was not slowing down because, in his mind, this is what led to Jasper coming on base, which led to them getting benched. "That was a lump that was very hard to swallow at the time, and it's even harder to swallow, now that evidence has suddenly gone missing."

"None of it has gone missing," Jasper declared, his tone calm. "Even if nobody else in this room had been there, it's been removed for safekeeping."

"*Safekeeping*," Sam repeated, with an eye roll. "In other words, brushed under the carpet."

"I don't think so," Jasper stated, "but it's definitely being handled by a higher pay grade than what you or any of the rest of us have at the moment."

The boss looked like he had been kicked in the teeth, but he held his gaze steady.

"That shouldn't be the way this works," Sam snapped, staring at Jasper in frustration. "We shouldn't have to bow to the bosses above who keep shit hidden. That's how this stuff happens and keeps happening."

"I won't argue with you about that," Jasper replied. "I'm

just telling you that the information involved has been removed and that your boss here knows about it."

"*Your boss,*" Morgan jumped on to that wording. "Meaning he's our boss but not yours?"

"At the moment, he is not," Jasper stated, without batting an eye. "At the moment, I'm answering to somebody else. And, if you don't think I still have to answer to them, then you don't have any understanding of how my phone calls and emails have been going of late," he shared, with a flat look toward Tristan.

Tristan nodded. "We all have to account for our actions. Whether you believe it or not, none of us gets to walk away from this free and clear."

"Yet you were there at the lab this morning. Why?"

"I anticipated that whoever knew about the missing evidence would go after it, so I requested to be on security detail for the lab. Still, I knew it would take a little bit to get put in place. So, I sat there and watched just in case, and I saw the gunman go in."

"So what?" Sam barked. "You decided, just like that, to go in after him? What the hell?"

"Of course I did. What kind of investigators are you who wouldn't go after a gunman?"

"We call for backup, for one thing," Sam declared in fury.

"I did call for backup," Tristan replied, "and then I went straight in because I didn't want to see the lab techs have to deal with a gunman, when none of the techs are equipped with weapons. Not to mention the fact that they aren't even trained on how to ask questions the way we are."

"So, you jumped right in, *huh?*" Sam asked, pressing on.

"Yeah, I did. I have a weapon, and I'm licensed to use

it," Tristan declared, his voice hard as he replied. "And I don't know what problem you've got rammed up your ass," he added, staring down at Sam, as his formerly cheerful aura burned away and was replaced with fury, "but you better get it out of there before it turns your attitude to shit." Sam was about to bark a reply when Tristan went on, "And, by the way, I don't have to explain my motives to you, and I sure as hell don't have to explain my actions. We all have people we report to, and you're not it." And, with that, he turned and walked into the office he'd been using and shut the door.

A few minutes later Jasper walked in and sat down across from him. "Don't let them get to you."

Tristan shrugged. "I shouldn't. I just don't understand why they're even still here."

"They're technically working their own hours at the moment. They just don't yet know that they're being moved," Jasper shared. "I'm sorry for that because it seems like it's all underhanded, and I don't understand why."

When Jasper hesitated, Tristan waved a hand. "I get it. I do. It wouldn't be happening if the brass didn't think it was needed," he said, with an eye roll.

"We've also not cleared them yet either."

"Of course we haven't cleared them," Tristan muttered. "That would be too easy, wouldn't it?"

"The problem is that nobody's making it easy," Jasper stated.

"Of course not, and, because of that, they will lose their jobs."

"No, they will be reassigned," Jasper corrected.

"Which means they're losing their jobs, their jobs right here that they may or may not have liked."

"But we will have a completely new department," Jasper

stated firmly. "Ever since I got assigned to investigate the attack on Mason, it's been one step forward and two back with this case. I'm not dealing with this rogue team on top of all that. So I'm letting the brass move slowly on these guys."

"What about their boss?" Tristan asked. "That comment blew up too."

"It sure did. Still was true though."

"It was true, but how long do we have to hold off?"

"Until this is done," Jasper replied. "That's what we're here for."

"Maybe so, but we're sure finding all kinds of other shit while we're at it."

"That's what happens, doesn't it? We dig, we dig, and we dig, and we find shit, more shit, and even more shit. Eventually the hope is that you find the plug that's stopping the sewer from draining." Jasper shrugged. "As soon as we do that, we'll be good to go." Just then Jasper's phone rang. "This is Tesla. I have to get it. … Hey, Tesla. Is everything okay?" he asked, with a certain urgency in his tone.

Even Tristan heard her crying over the phone.

"He's awake, Jasper. Mason's awake," she cried out. "He's awake."

Jasper grinned and looked over at Tristan.

Tristan waved Jasper on. "Go on," Tristan said. "Go talk to Mason. He's the one who's likely to give us the best help out of all this."

"I hope so." Jasper noted, "because the alternative is that he knows nothing."

"One thing," Tristan added, with a note of warning in his tone, just as Jasper went to leave the room. "You've also got to consider that he might not remember anything. Not yet."

Jasper nodded. "I'm ignoring that aspect for now and just am happy he's awake."

"Good, because head injuries can be a problem."

"Not only that but Mason's other wounds as well. I'll let you know as soon as I hear anything more." And, with that, Jasper raced from the room.

Tristan sat for a long moment, a smile on his face, thinking how amazing it would be if Mason made it through this. Aside from all the obvious reasons that they needed him to make it, *everybody* needed him to. They needed the reassurance that, at least sometimes, when it counted, the good guys won.

CHAPTER 6

AMARYLIS STAYED IN her office and worked through the rest of the day. Such a weird energy filled the place now. She kept looking up, looking around, looking for something off, but everything seemed calm. Several times Dr. Cox had walked by, asking if she was okay.

Every time she'd nodded, then smiled and said, "Yeah, I'm fine. How about you?"

One time he shrugged and admitted, "It feels weird." Then he slapped the doorframe and walked away. But he was right. It did feel weird. All of this felt weird. Like something brewed underneath, a sense of waiting, a sense of something coming down the pipeline that they wouldn't like. Still, it was there in front of them, just not yet close enough to see.

She considered what Tristan had mentioned earlier about the possibility of whoever was a part of this coming back again. She didn't know whether anybody would attempt to get inside the lab again or believed the material had been moved. What she did know was that she didn't want any part of it.

She wasn't even sure how she got involved in the first place, except that she was the one who had found the unusual USB key and had recognized it for what it was. She wondered what would have happened if that much had stayed in the realm of mystery. It might have been a good thing, or it might have been worse. Considering the information that was found on it, even the little she knew about, it was enough to keep her worried about opening Pandora's box.

When she finally got to the end of her shift, she looked in on Dr. Cox, still working in his office, but the techs had all gone home, which seemed disturbing. She got up and entered his office and waited while he finished a call. When he got off the phone, she asked, "Are you ready to leave?"

He nodded. "We should be out of here by now, shouldn't we?" He looked around with a sigh. "It still seems weird though."

"The whole day has been that way, and I don't know about you, but I'm ready to have it over with."

He laughed, then suddenly looked surprised. "Have you been waiting for me to leave?"

She shrugged. "I don't know if I've been waiting for you to leave as much as, … uh, looking to have you leave with me," she shared, with a wry look.

"Oh, shit, yeah. I never even thought of that. And we do have security out there, right?"

"Supposedly." She nodded.

He grabbed his coat and asked, "When you say, *supposedly*, what are you thinking?"

She shrugged. "I would like to think that security is out there, but we haven't seen anybody and we haven't been introduced to anyone, so who knows?"

He nodded. "Let's go. I'm ready to get home anyway."

"You live alone?"

"I live alone," he confirmed. "As I told you, it's been

about six months now since my wife passed. It took a long time to get used to it, but I've gradually gotten there. I won't say I particularly like living alone, not after being happily married all those years"—he shook his head—"but the adjustment is freeing in a way. I just don't know what comes next."

"I don't imagine any of us do," she murmured.

"And you're alone," he stated point-blank. "That might be a state you would care to change."

"Maybe," she murmured. "I'm not exactly sure what I want to do at this point."

"Good enough," he replied. "We don't have to make any decisions right away, but I'm glad you're here. So please don't leave this position too quickly. Finding you was hard enough."

She chuckled. "I don't think it was that bad."

"Oh, it was worse than you think," he shared. "It's not easy to find qualified people for these positions."

"Hell, I'm not even sure I knew what it would entail."

"Normally it's peaceful. We work with the dead, so how much ruckus can they cause?" he asked, half joking.

She smiled. "A lot of people just don't understand that."

"Nope. A friend of mine wanted to set me up on a blind date after my wife passed away, and it wasn't that long ago," he added, shaking his head. "I guess she didn't tell the poor lady in question what I did for a living. So, when she heard, she must have been pretty freaked out because she went to the washroom and never came back."

Amarylis frowned in shock and then burst out laughing. "On the other hand," she pointed out, "she may have saved you a lot of heartache from going down a pathway with her, only to find out later she couldn't handle it. At least this way you got an honest response."

"Yeah," he agreed, "but wow. What a response was that? I tell you that my ego took quite a hit."

She was still chuckling as she shook her head, while they slowly walked toward the exit. "That wasn't on you," Amarylis said. "That was on your friend."

"Maybe, and she did apologize profusely the next day, surprised that her girlfriend was still pretty freaked out about the whole thing."

"It's not as if you are a serial killer. Somebody needs to do this job and do it properly. While it takes a special person to handle this profession, it's nothing to be ridiculed about," she protested. "That's just silly."

"That's what I thought, but, hey, you never know what people are thinking."

"Now you know," she pointed out, "and she made it very clear."

He winced at that. "I could have done with a little less clarity," he noted. "I was pretty depressed by the time I got home, after I finally realized she wasn't coming back."

"And that's the embarrassing part," Amarylis stated. "You're sitting there at a restaurant, waiting for somebody who never shows up again."

"Exactly, and I haven't been on a date since." He tossed her a mock look. "But you, young lady, should be out on dates."

"Ha, but not right now. Not while this mess is going on."

"Are you sure?" he asked in a teasing voice. "That Tristan fellow seemed awfully serious about you. I can definitely predict, with some degree of certainty, that something is happening there."

She rolled her eyes at that. "We'll see. ... He's nice enough, but I'm not sure how much of what appears to be interest is because of his job."

Cox's tone went serious as he replied, "The looks I saw him cast in your direction had nothing to do with the job, but I can understand how you would want to make sure. You don't want to end up alone at some restaurant, like me."

She smiled. The front door loomed ahead of them. As she looked around, she frowned. "I don't see any sign of security."

"The guards should be inside and outside," Cox declared, glancing around.

As they got to the front door, she pushed it open and stepped outside. Almost immediately she felt this weird sensation in the air. She hesitated, then jumped back inside.

Dr. Cox hadn't made it outside yet. "What was that all about?"

"I don't know," she said, "but I don't like it." Slowly he turned toward the door, then back to her. She nodded.

Dr. Cox frowned. "Are you sure you're not just freaked out about what happened earlier today? It's not as if you wouldn't have good reason," he pointed out.

"No, it's not that." She frowned, shoving her hands into her pockets as she stared outside.

"So, what do you want to do, stay here all night? Surely we must leave at some point," Cox said in a partially joking tone.

She looked up at him. "Do you want to take a chance?"

"Not particularly," he muttered, thinking about it. "Call that partner of yours and see if he knows anything about the security."

She pulled out her phone and phoned Tristan.

When he answered, his voice was distracted, but he seemed happy to hear from her. "You missed me?"

She ignored him and went straight to the point. "Did you ever get security set up out here?"

"Why? What's up?"

"I want to leave the building and had this weird feeling, so I came back inside. Now I feel like a prisoner."

"Hang on a minute. I'll get right back to you. And please don't move." With that, he ended the call.

She stared down at the phone and shrugged. "He told me to stay here, and he would get back to me."

"Good," Dr. Cox replied. "At least then you'll feel better. A little bit of security goes a long way."

"A whole lot of security," she corrected him, "goes a lot further." Cox just smiled at that.

When Tristan called her back a few minutes later, he stated, "I'm not getting an answer from the security guard, so hold tight. I'm on my way. Don't leave the building. Just stay inside and keep away from the windows."

"What if somebody else wants to come in?" she asked in a freaked-out tone.

"Don't let them in. Not even if you see someone you know. Just confirm that the doors are locked and stay there. I'll be there as soon as I can."

She frowned at that, looked over at Dr. Cox, and repeated what Tristan had told her. "We're to stay inside, keep away from the windows, and don't let anybody else in no matter what."

"What are we to do about visitors?" he asked. "It is a public building."

"Maybe, but it is after-hours. Plus, haven't you noticed how deserted it feels right now?"

"I have." He nodded, looking around. "Let's step back away from the glass doors."

"Yeah, good idea," she muttered, and they stepped back enough so that they were not visible from the outside. As they stood in the shadows and waited, she asked, "Is it possible that people are still after that key?"

"If anybody has reason to believe something very important is on that USB key," Dr. Cox began, "I highly doubt they will give up so easily."

"So, one dead body isn't enough," she stated bitterly.

"I think we will find the body count doesn't matter to these people. Once you've killed the first time, every time thereafter gets easier." She frowned at him, and he nodded. "Yeah, I've got lots of military experience myself," he added, "and it wasn't my thing."

"Yet you're still here."

"I didn't like the shooting part." He chuckled at that. "I would much rather work on the bodies after the fact, which is where I'm at now." He sighed. "You don't forget your days dealing with the fighting, but at least now I'm happy being where I'm at."

"I'm happy for you," she murmured. "That couldn't have been easy."

"No, it sure wasn't. Not only was it not easy, sometimes those memories just never leave you." He gave her a jaded look, shaking his head. "My wife used to say that I slept about two hours every night, but I was always surprised she thought I slept even that much."

"It was that bad?"

"Sometimes it was." He nodded. "Sometimes there's just nothing you can do, and those memories roll through your head all the time, even forty years later."

She winced at that. "That means you were there when you were very young."

He laughed. "Signed up as soon as I could, ever the fool." As he finished his story, headlights flashed across the front of the building.

She hesitated, waiting to see if it was Tristan, but Cox pulled her back. "We're supposed to stay out of the way of the windows," he reminded her.

"I was just hoping it was him."

"If it's Tristan, he will let you know," Cox stated, and they waited a little bit longer.

When no phone call came, she groaned. "So, it's not him."

"Doesn't seem to be. You know very well that, if it were him, he would be contacting you."

So they waited, the minutes ticking by slowly.

Just then her phone rang. She answered it in a hurry. "Tristan?"

"Yes, it's me. I'm just walking outside the building."

"A vehicle shone its lights on the front door a few minutes ago," she shared, "but we couldn't see who it was."

"And it could have been completely innocent too," Dr. Cox reminded her at her side.

Tristan echoed that sentiment. "It could have been nothing, but I have not seen the security guard. I have two other men on their way as well."

"So, what do you want us to do?" she asked. "We could go back up to our office, if you think that's necessary."

"It might be. Give me a few minutes." And, with that, he hung up.

Amarylis filled in Dr. Cox. "Tristan is walking toward the front of the building and asked for a few minutes."

"He's probably looking for the security guard." Cox crossed his arms and leaned against the wall. "Let's hope he's not dead too."

She groaned. "That would be terrible."

"Not only that," Cox added, with a hard mocking grin, "can you imagine calling in our forensics team again?"

She shook her head. "They would not be happy."

"No, they sure wouldn't be, and honestly, with good reason. None of us have gotten a whole lot of sleep since this mess started," he muttered. "We all want it to end, just not this way."

"No, of course not," she agreed. "Still, it seems as if you've got a good team here."

"I do. I've been working with them for a long time, at least most of them."

"When you say *most*, not everybody?"

"No, a couple guys are pretty new," he muttered, as he gave her a look, "but *new* doesn't mean bad."

"No, it doesn't mean bad. I just wondered who the new ones are." When he mentioned the one that she rarely had anything to do with, she nodded. "That explains why he never speaks to me."

"He's only been here about a month, and then we have Adam, our newest hire," Cox noted. "He's only been here for a few weeks. He came in just before you."

She stared at him in astonishment.

"What is that look for?"

"I wasn't expecting that, as he seems to be fairly well adapted."

"Yeah, I think he is," Cox agreed, tilting his head as he considered it. "He took to it very easily in fact."

"Suspiciously so?" she asked.

His eyebrows climbing, Cox replied, "I hope not. ... Are you tearing apart our staff now too?"

"No, not necessarily. I just don't know what compromising material these bad guys might have on various people."

"That's a good point," Cox admitted. "I never thought of it that way."

"We don't want to think about it now if we don't have to," she shared, "and investigating our own staff sucks."

"I've never had to do that," Cox replied, "but you're right. It would be bad. Especially when I've known most of these guys for a long time."

"And the trouble is, when you've known them for a long time, you tend to think that you *know* them and that they're free and clear from any investigation," she explained in a hushed voice, "and that can be a fatal error."

"Ouch," Cox muttered. "I don't think I like this conversation."

"No, I don't either," she confirmed. Her phone buzzed just then, and she looked down at her incoming text. "It's Tristan."

"Is he coming in?"

"He says for us to just stay where we are."

Cox frowned at that. "Does that mean he found something?"

She quickly phoned Tristan, and, when he answered, she asked impatiently, "What aren't you telling me?"

He groaned and relented, "I found the guard. He's alive but not in very good shape. I've got an ambulance coming."

"Let us see to him." When Tristan hesitated, she reminded him, "Hello, we're doctors, not just of dead people, so if need be—"

Immediately he replied, "Come on out then. I'm not

sure we can do anything for him here though."

THE TWO CORONERS raced to the downed guard, as Tristan watched. The guard moaned softly, but he was breathing, and it looked to be more of a head injury than anything. Amarylis dropped to her knees, and Tristan watched as she did a quick and thorough exam of the guard. "What's the ETA on the ambulance?" she asked Tristan.

"I would have thought they would be here by now," he said in frustration, and just then they heard the wail of a siren in the distance.

She stepped back and announced, "He's been conked on the back of the head."

"Yeah, that was my take on it too." Tristan turned to Dr. Cox. "I presume your opinion is the same?"

Dr. Cox was still examining the poor man, but he nodded. "That is my estimate as well. I don't know what the hell is going on around here, but *this*, ... damn it, this is getting ugly. It also means that we can't leave," he added, with a sigh.

"You can," Amarylis suggested, turning to Dr. Cox. "I will stay here."

Cox frowned. "Why the hell would you want to stay here?"

"Because, until security is in place," she pointed out, "everything here is in danger of being destroyed."

Cox hesitated, then groaned. "You're right, ... damn it."

"I have security coming," Tristan shared. "It will take a few minutes to get the team here, particularly now that we have evidence of another attack."

"You need more than one guy though," she declared, turning to look at him, frowning. "These men are getting picked off, one by one."

He nodded. "That was my argument earlier, and you're right. We do need at least two at a time, but it's also a matter of the budget."

"Budget? … Screw that," she cried out. "These men deserve better."

Tristan smiled at her passionate response. "We are looking after them, you know."

"Maybe, but this guy, he didn't get looked after, and we need to make sure that he lives. He might not be right in the head, for all we know."

The ambulance pulled up at that moment, parked, and the driver raced to them, while the passenger ran to the back to get the gurney. The first paramedic noted the two doctors, before dropping to his knees to check out the patient. "Good Christ, no end to this now, is there?"

Dr. Cox grumbled, "I keep telling Tristan to stop bringing me patients. So I guess he decided to send them your way instead." As bad jokes went, it did the job, and it did lighten the sad atmosphere, at least for a moment.

In ten minutes, the guard was loaded up and gone.

Tristan turned to the two coroners. "Now, when was the last time you saw the guard?"

She shook her head. "As I mentioned earlier to Dr. Cox, we had absolutely no contact with him. We didn't know who was here, when he came, where he was positioned, or anything else."

Tristan frowned at that. "He was supposed to report in, at least when the shift changed."

He turned to Dr. Cox, who shook his head. "I don't

know what he was supposed to do, but I can tell you, young man, I never saw this guard before."

Tristan shook his head. "I didn't handle the shift change, but we should have new men coming any minute."

"As long as they don't become new fodder for the meat grinder," Dr. Cox muttered.

"Let's hope not." Tristan shot him a hard look. "These are good men, and they're here for the best of reasons."

When the new guard drove in, he had three others with him.

"I hope they're all staying," Dr. Cox declared. "We don't want anybody else hurt." As it was, all four men were guards for this shift, and they were scheduled for a shift change in a few hours with another four.

With that completed, Tristan looked over at her. "Are you okay?"

She nodded. "I am. It just feels very odd and sad to see this happen. We've had a fairly routine work life, up until this."

"*Fairly*," Dr. Cox teased her. "It was a nice, quiet work life, and all our patients came in without any arguments." He shook his head. "I will go home and grab some sleep. At the rate we're going, tomorrow will be another shit show."

They watched as he got into his vehicle and drove off. Tristan turned to her and asked, "What about you? You ready to go home?"

"Not particularly, but it's probably the safest place for me."

He nodded. "I won't argue with that, but I would suggest dinner first."

She nodded. "Are we talking about dinner out or picking up dinner and taking it back to my place?"

"That's an option too," he noted. "Which would you prefer? Besides, you're the one who's worked all day."

She laughed. "Are you telling me that you didn't?"

He flashed her a bright grin. "Yeah, but this is what I do."

"Sure, and I worked on bodies all day. I am a little tired, but it would be nice to get out and to see something other than the inside of my apartment."

"Done. Particularly after we didn't even get to have pizza out."

"We got pizza," she corrected, with an eye roll, "just not exactly in the atmosphere we thought it would be."

"Very true, so let's go try something else." He led her to his car and then asked, "Do you want to drive home first and leave your vehicle there or go together from here and come back?"

She frowned as if contemplating the options. "I think I would rather have my wheels with me, than to leave them here."

"Good enough. You drive, and I'll follow."

And that's what they did. By the time they got to her place, she was calm and settled enough to sort out what she wanted to do for dinner. When he approached her car, she got out and locked it up. "I want Italian."

"Italian, as in not pizza?"

"Italian, as in not pizza," she repeated, with a laugh. "Pasta would be good."

"Pasta is doable," he said, with a smile. "I do know a good pasta place."

"I suspect," she replied, with a laugh, "you know a lot of places."

He shrugged. "Maybe. I've lived in this area for quite a

while, so you do eventually get to know every eatery, ranking them as you go." She just snorted and didn't say anything. "Unless you meant something completely different."

She shrugged. "I was just thinking that a guy like you must have lots of girlfriends."

He laughed. "No, I sure don't," he argued, yet still cheerful, which seemed to be his personality. "I'm not necessarily somebody who likes to do the quick-fling thing. I did that for a few years when I was young and stupid, but I've grown up a lot, and life changes, so ..."

"That doesn't mean you don't have or haven't had serious relationships," she pointed out.

"No, and I've had a couple of those, just not any that went the distance."

She got into his vehicle, and he drove carefully to a small restaurant. It was bigger than the hole-in-the-wall pizza place, but it was definitely more of an intimate setting.

"What happened to your relationships?" she asked.

"I got close to asking one to marry me, but then she decided she wanted to go travel for a few years, see more of life, wasn't ready to settle down. It was almost as if she knew I was getting ready to ask."

"She probably did, instincts and all that, you know. She quite possibly saved you a lot more heartache."

"Maybe so," he conceded, "though it did take a fair bit to get over it."

"Of course. Rejection like that is never easy. And the second one?"

He shrugged. "We were just too busy, and we drifted apart. She's now happily married to what seems to be a great guy. She has a couple kids, and I'm happy for her."

"Good. That means you're not holding a torch for anyone."

He laughed. "No, definitely not." He parked, hopped out, then went around and opened the door for her.

She smiled up at him. "I'm not used to seeing manners like these."

"My mama would have my head on a platter if I didn't treat a lady right," he stated in a sardonic tone.

"I'm not sure your mama was all that wrong, but there are women who prefer to flout their independence and all that," Amarylis noted. "Still, I find it lovely to be treated like I'm something special."

He smiled and led her inside the restaurant. "Don't you ever doubt it. You are something special."

CHAPTER 7

TRISTAN'S COMMENT SURPRISED Amarylis, but more than that was the sincerity behind it. Once inside, they were met by a waitress. He smiled, but it was a congenial smile, the type you would use with almost anyone. They were seated at the back, where lit candles were part of the decor. She smiled at the romantic setting. "Now this feels like a date."

He pulled off his jacket and draped it over his chair. "Okay, it's a date then."

"Is it though?" she asked, with half a smile in his direction. "It's not as if we're dating."

"But maybe we are," he stated cheerfully. "Maybe you just didn't get the memo." She burst out laughing at that. "So, we are treating this as a date," he announced. He sat across from her and smiled. "Besides, why shouldn't we take a few moments in all this chaos to enjoy ourselves?"

She didn't know what to say to that, but recognizing that she did want to view this as a date, she wouldn't argue. "Thank you. It's nice to find a bit of normalcy in this world gone nuts."

"It is, indeed. How is Dr. Cox doing?"

She shrugged. "He seems to be mostly okay, though you

never know with him. He seems to take things in stride, but I think he internalizes a lot of it, then doesn't know how to let it go."

"Most people don't, you know," he replied. "You get into a stressful situation, do the best you can, then hope there's enough time for everything to sink in and to change all on its own."

"Maybe," she murmured. "It's definitely a strange scenario involving Mason's shooting."

"It is, but it's more or less over."

As an answer, Amarylis felt it was more of a *toss it out there* response, hoping she wouldn't delve any deeper, but that wasn't her style. The waitress came before Amarylis could address that issue, so she held off as they placed their orders, until the woman disappeared. She asked, "Do you think it is over?" He hesitated, and she waited to see what he would say. When he shook his head, she smiled. "Thank you."

"For what?" he asked, with a smile.

"For not treating me like some bimbo who just needed an answer to make her happy. I'm all about finding the truth, even if it isn't a truth I particularly wish to find."

"You and me both," he agreed. "It's just that a lot of people aren't used to the truth, and don't like it when it rears its ugly head."

"That's very true, but I deal in the truth, whether people like it or not. It's a part of my job that I'm acutely aware of and that people prefer to hide from."

"Sad, isn't it?"

"Yet it allows everybody to live their life," she noted. "A life where they don't have to face the effects of everything that you and I deal with—you with the living horrors and me with the dead ones."

He smiled at that. "That's a good way to look at it. I'm sure you get a lot more routine cases than this current one, with all the dead bodies surrounding Mason's shooting."

"I do. I get a lot of normal cases, and normal is good. Though in Chicago, normal was a very different term."

"I'm sure deaths from shootings, gang fights, and murders were part of your regular daily business there."

"Absolutely, and sometimes there are no good answers, but you still do everything you can. You know, like when the ER fixes somebody up, sends them back out, and still they end up on my table within a few weeks." She shook her head. "That happened more than a couple times."

"That in itself must be frustrating," Tristan noted, "and a circle that's so hard to break, but it's not just our problem. It's a global issue these days."

"It's an everybody problem because it's almost always either gang or drug related," she shared. Then she shrugged. "This is another reason why people of our professions don't normally have dates. This conversation is one that most people can't handle."

He smiled at her. "I'm sure you've already recognized that I'm not most people."

She laughed at that. "Now that I know you're not most people, and you've had a couple close brushes with marriage," she added, "tell me more about yourself. Tell me about your family, your friendships, your childhood."

"Any particular reason?" he asked, eyeing her.

She shrugged. "I just want to know more about you, the real you, not necessarily the you I've been seeing at work up until now."

"That is the real me, you know?"

"It absolutely is," she agreed, with a smile, "and I get that. That's the protective you. That's the man who's always on duty, but what about the child where that man came from? What sent you into this … field?" She waved her hand, not understanding exactly what his field even was.

He sat back, and, when their waitress delivered a glass of wine, he slowly twirled it in his hands and told her his life story. When it finally came to an end, he took a sip of his wine and admitted, "Wow, I haven't talked that much about myself in a very long time."

"I wonder if you ever talk about yourself that much," she teased.

"No, I don't. It's not considered to be good manners."

"I'm the one who asked," she protested.

"Maybe." He gave a shake of his head.

She realized that he was a bit on the shy side. She smiled and patted his hand. "I love the fact that you have siblings and that you were a typical terror growing up. I'm sure your parents are very proud of you."

"I think so," he said, with a smile, "but I also know they live in fear that someday they will get that phone call that tells them I'm not coming home again."

As someone who's dealt with making those phone calls, she nodded. "The thing is, that's a phone call that can come at anytime, anyplace, and for any reason," she shared. "It doesn't necessarily have anything to do with the work you do."

"That's debatable."

"Sure, you've certainly got a heightened number of things that could go wrong in your world, but it wouldn't be because of that as much as the reality that we're all heading to the same place."

"It's comforting to think that though," he replied, with a chuckle. "I was very close to my grandmother, and, when she passed away, I found it very, very difficult. … Then I had this moment of an almost peaceful passing in my head, where I heard her telling me to be good and that she would be watching over me."

Amarylis smiled. "I've heard stories like that before. I think it's wonderful, and, for whatever reason that these things happen, either for your sake or for hers, I think it helps all of us in the end."

"I can imagine the horror in that too," he admitted, as he lifted his wineglass. "What about you?"

"Oh, dear, are you sure it isn't time for food?"

He laughed at that. "No, absolutely not. Come on. Talk to me."

So, she filled him in on her childhood, which compared to his was lonely and empty. She shrugged. "My dad was a doctor, who ended up in pathology."

"Is that why you went into it?"

She shook her head. "No, but I always had a fascination with the dead," she murmured, and the conversation carried on between them.

With dinner well underway, a relaxing peaceful atmosphere had settled between the two of them. She laughed when they were almost done. "Maybe we didn't intend for this to be a date, but it ended up nice regardless," she shared.

"I'm glad you enjoyed it," he replied, with a warm smile. "And you're right. It morphed into a nice date, but I intended to ask you out at some point anyway."

She shrugged. "That's nice to know."

"Hey, it's not all business."

"Maybe not, but it feels like a lot of it is."

"That's just because of the crazy circumstances we find ourselves in at the moment, but good things are on the way."

"Oh, I'm glad to hear that," she said, chuckling, "because it's been a pretty rough go so far." Then she asked, "How is your friend doing?"

"The one in the hospital?"

"Yes, Tesla's husband."

"Apparently he woke up today, but I don't know how he is doing. I haven't had an update from Jasper yet. I was hoping for one but haven't had any news, which is concerning."

"If he just woke up after all this time in a coma, chances are he may have gone right back under almost immediately. It takes a lot of energy for a body to heal from that kind of an injury, and he's got to be on powerful medications as well."

"I guess I was just hoping for an update and some good news."

"Maybe Jasper can't give you an update because there isn't one to give." Tristan smiled at her, and she just laughed. "I get it. I probably sound like I'm constantly smoothing things over and making everything seem as if it'll all work out."

"It's not a bad trait," he pointed out.

"Maybe not, but sometimes I think it's more of a peacemaking trait."

"Which, considering you didn't have any siblings," Tristan noted, "is an interesting trait for you to have."

"I may not have had any siblings," she conceded, "but my parents weren't exactly the kind to get along."

"But I thought you just had your dad."

"My mom was in the picture, just not very often, so he

had custody and raised me," she explained.

"Ah, so there's the other side of that childhood."

"Yep, there's always another side, isn't there?" When they finally got up to leave, his phone rang.

He looked down at it and frowned. "They have good timing, don't they?"

"I don't know about good timing," she acknowledged as they walked outside, "but it is interesting when you consider that we just finished an entire meal. We should be thankful they let you eat properly for once."

"Exactly. It's my boss." He answered the call. "Jasper." Tristan walked out beside her, his hand on her lower back, guiding her through the crowd that was just coming in. "How's Mason?"

She couldn't hear all the conversation, but it continued for a few more minutes. When he got off the phone, he nodded. "You were right. He was back asleep again once Jasper got there. Still, Mason was awake long enough to confirm that he should be okay."

"At least he's taken a turn for the better," Amarylis pointed out, "though I would be cautious about celebrating too much, too soon."

Tristan winced. "Let's not tell them that. Tesla and Jasper were pretty well counting on this being a fairly positive note."

"It is a firmly positive note," Amarylis confirmed. "I never said it wasn't. I'm just more of a cautious person."

"Right, well again, let's keep it more promising than cautious," he suggested, with a smile. "Everybody is hoping Mason will recover just fine."

"And he probably will. Keep that thought anyway."

As they settled into his car, he asked, "Are you ready to

go home?"

"I don't know about ready to go home, but I probably should. It's been a stressful few days, so some good sleep would help a lot."

"Good enough. And you're not nervous at all in your place, are you?"

"No, I haven't been," she replied, "and I don't want you making me nervous either."

He laughed. "Not my intention at all. Let's just get you home."

As he drove up to her place, she asked, "Do you think it's safe for us now at the morgue, or should we expect to have more issues?"

"I don't know about *expecting* more issues," he replied, "but I certainly hope our beefed-up security would discourage others at this point."

"But we don't know for sure, do we?"

"No, of course not," he said. "We have a higher dead body count than we expected as well, which is never a good sign."

"*Right.*" She winced. "Can't say I expected that either."

"No." He smiled at her. "Anyway I'll walk you up and confirm everything is okay, if you don't mind." She nodded her consent. As they took the stairs to her apartment, he asked, "What was your day at the office like? And how was Dr. Cox?"

"He was fine, until it came time to leave. I think he's lonely," she shared, sorrow in her tone.

"In what way?"

"He lost his wife several months back," she replied, "and he hasn't gotten back out into the real world of the living."

"No, especially after a happy marriage—at least I presume it was a happy marriage," he said, glancing at her. "I'm sure that's got to be a tough thing to handle."

"He's a good man though, and everybody there appreciates him. They all seem to like working with him, and there hasn't been very much in the way of turnover. So I think that makes him a good boss."

"Yeah, either that or he threatens them," Tristan teased, with a laugh.

"Oh, I don't imagine so." At her door, she turned and said, "Thank you for dinner. It was a lovely evening."

"It was, but I'm still coming in and checking out your place."

Wordless, unable to respond, and wondering how the hell she got here, she opened the door and led him in. Sure enough, he walked right through the entire place and then came back to her. "Good enough."

She had to laugh. "You are concerned, aren't you? You try hard not to show it, but you're still concerned."

"It's not that I'm concerned or that I am not concerned," he replied, with a cheerful smile. "I call it being cautious, since there's been way too much going on. Now, when I leave, … you lock that door. Got it?"

"Got it," she said, a twinkle in her gaze.

"I'm glad you can laugh about it," he noted. "That means the upsets of the last few days haven't been too rough on you."

"No, and I hope that they don't become any worse," she noted, with a smile.

He nodded. "You know what I will do now, don't you?"

Her eyebrows shot up. "No, I'm not exactly sure what you will do at all." She frowned at him, but his smile deepened, and he leaned forward and kissed her ever-so-

softly. "And then you still look at me with surprise on your face."

"The surprise," she began, finding her words, "was that it was only half a kiss." He laughed as she proceeded to give her full argument. "If you are kissing somebody good night, you should do it properly." And, with that, she wrapped her arms around his neck, pulled his head down, and laid a kiss on him with all the heart and passion she could muster. When she stepped back a few moments later, delighted at the cross-eyed look on his face, she whispered, "Now *that's* a proper good night."

And then she shut the door in his face.

TRISTAN WALKED OUT to his car, turned, and stared at the sky. He had a silly grin on his face, but, for the life of him, he couldn't wipe it off. If she hadn't closed her door on him, he would have walked right back in and given her a real kiss, and that was still on his mind. Instead he stood here outside, looking like an idiot. With a headshake, he turned back to his car, and, as he went to open his door, he heard an odd sound.

He crouched down, turned to look back where the sound had come from. Something disturbed him. Maybe the thought of a bullet wheezing past his head. As he sat in the parking lot, he heard a whisper.

"We need to go in."

With his head tilted, Tristan slowly crept around his car, until he could see two guys sitting on the ground beside a car, smoking a cigarette. He studied the two men but didn't recognize either of them.

One looked at his watch and whispered, "She should be home by now."

With those words out of his mouth, Tristan's heart froze. He realized that a lot of other females surely lived in this apartment building, but he doubted that very many of them would be mixed up in something that would necessitate guys sitting around, waiting for them.

"Maybe we should give her a little longer."

"How the hell long can she take?"

"She might have had a date or something."

"Who would date her?" One guy snarled. "Nobody wants her. She deals with bodies all day, … dead bodies, and that's just gross."

That sealed it for Tristan. He moved farther away from those two and phoned her.

"What's up?" she asked, a smile in her tone. "What is it now? Was it that kiss?"

"That kiss was enough to knock me on my six," he replied in a bare whisper, "but then I heard two guys out here, talking about waiting a few more minutes before they come up and visit you, hoping you'll be back now."

"They may be talking about someone else," she pointed out, but panic clearly rose in her tone.

"That could be, but I doubt many other gals in your building deal with dead bodies all day long. When one of them suggested that you might be out on a date, the other made it quite clear that he thought it was disgusting that anybody would date someone who dealt with bodies all day."

She sucked in her breath. "Who are these men?"

"I don't know, but I will find out. Now, you stay put, and, unless you hear my voice at your door, you don't open it. Got it?"

"What are you doing?"

"Leave that to me, and I'll call you as soon as I know more." And, with that, he quickly ended the call. Not wanting to take the chance of more things happening that he couldn't control, he quickly texted Jasper about this trouble in Amarylis's parking lot. Then he pulled out his weapon and headed to where the men were. His heart froze when he noted they were gone. Somehow they had slipped away.

He raced back to the building and headed up to her apartment. When he got there, he called out to her.

She opened the door and frowned. "What was that all about?"

"Get in," he snapped, quickly closing the door behind him. He leaned his back against the door and took a deep breath. "I lost them in the parking lot." She paled as she stared at him. He nodded. "So, my assumption is that they're on their way up here."

"In that case, I'm glad you came back." Her words faded slightly, as she turned to stare at the door behind him.

"Yeah, me too," he murmured. "Now we have to figure out how to deal with two of them."

She shook her head. "I still don't understand why they are interested in me."

"I think somebody knows that you found the USB key or that the key was held there at the forensics lab, and you work nearby. I hate to say this, but, out of everybody, you probably look like the easiest option, someone more likely to cooperate without giving them too much trouble."

"Easiest option? I can take them back to the lab—which obviously if it came to that I would—but what are they expecting to find there?"

"Answers, and, if you don't give it to them, they will try

and get it from you."

She paled as she understood. "What the hell did I get myself into with this job?"

"I don't think it's the job," Tristan noted in a calm tone, "although I can see how that might be your first instinct. I'm pretty damn sure it's whatever the hell else is going on," he shared, with a smile. Just then he heard a noise on the other side of the door, so he pulled her back slightly. When she stared at him in horror, he nodded. "We need to catch these guys alive," he whispered. "If they go back outside emptyhanded, and they were expected to come back with you, they may get shot dead. So look at us capturing them as doing them a big favor."

"We need to let Jasper in. He's downstairs."

"It could be Jasper but …"

She frowned at him. "Are you expecting that he'll get followed?"

"I don't know, but we're not taking any chances." Sure enough, a knock came on her door a few minutes later, and he heard Jasper's voice on the other side. She opened the door to let him in, only to find him being pushed forward, a gun at his back. The man behind him slammed shut her door.

"Ah, Tristan," she called out, although he was standing just behind her.

"Yeah, what's up?"

She pointed. "We've got a problem."

He looked up to see Jasper staring at him.

Jasper grimaced. "Sorry, this one caught me just outside in the hallway."

Tristan nodded, noting the code for *I only saw one*.

Then the gunman slammed his weapon into the side of

Jasper's head, and he dropped just inside her apartment. The gunman stood, staring at Amarylis, with a grin on his face. "It took two of us and one prisoner to get in here," he stated, with a slimy smile, "but I'm here now, and you can bet I'm not leaving without answers."

Tristan crossed his arms over his chest and glared at the new arrival. "I see you know how to make yourself real popular," he murmured.

"I don't give a shit about making myself popular or not. I want that damn key, and I want it now."

At his side, Amarylis stepped forward and announced, "Look. We don't have the damn key." Her tone of voice revealed her pent-up frustration. "What the fucking hell is with that key? If you would listen to the guys that you've sent beforehand, instead of just killing them, you would understand that. The key went into forensics, got locked up, and then it was removed," she shared in an exasperated tone, "and we don't know by whom or how or where it's even gone."

He grimaced. "At least that sounds more like the truth."

"It is the truth," she declared. "So why don't you guys believe us?"

"Because people want that key, and it doesn't matter what you say. Nobody'll believe you because they want it too badly."

"Why is it you want that key?" Tristan asked. "Seems to be a ton of interest in this, so maybe it should go to the highest bidder."

At that, the gun turned quickly in Tristan's direction. "So, is that what this is about then? You just want money for it?" he asked, with that same smarmy smile. "If that's the case, we can talk. Of course I would have thought a bullet in your head would have been enough of a payment, and negotiating *not* putting that bullet in your head will become your bargaining chip."

"Maybe." Tristan shrugged. "I'm not saying that I have any access to this damn key, but it seems like a lot of people want it pretty badly. So it must have something pretty interesting on it." The gunman glared at him, and Tristan snorted. "You can't argue the fact that we have a lot of interest here."

"I don't care what you've got," he snapped. "It's not for you to wonder."

"Jeez, are you serious? Think about what you just said."

"I don't have to think about it. I already know what I said, and you can just forget about the damn key."

"I would love to, but shits like you keep showing up because of all this interest in what's on that key," he replied, keeping his tone cool, as he watched the gunman's movements, while having a peripheral view of Jasper. He just moved ever-so-slightly, which was enough to know he was alive but possibly not enough to help them in this situation.

"You don't get to take an interest in anything. You will now forget about the damn thing."

"We would love to," Amarylis snapped, glaring at him. "But you people keep forgetting that we don't have it. We don't have access to it, and we can't get access to it."

"Why can't you?" he asked, pointing the gun at her.

"Because it was taken out of evidence, and we don't know by whom, we can't tell you who's got it."

The gunman glared at them in frustration. "The problem is, … I almost freaking believe you. It would be just so typical of this whole nightmare."

"If there's anything else we can help you with," she suggested, taking it down as notch, "we would, but we don't know what's going on with this damn key, except that a hell of a lot of people want it."

He nodded but didn't say anything, just staring off in the distance, as if sorting out something in his head. He turned his gaze back to her and added, "You seem to be the more sensible one, so maybe I'll take you with me." And he motioned at her to move.

Immediately Tristan stepped in front of her and stated, "You're not taking her anywhere." His voice was quiet, but the threat in his tone confirmed he meant every word.

The gunman laughed. "You do see what I'm holding in my hand, right?"

"I don't give a shit. How many guys are you all planning on killing before this is over?"

The gunman stared back. "As many as it takes. You are obviously too dense to get what's going on here, aren't you?"

"What? So you can stop being blackmailed, or so you can go blackmail somebody else?" Tristan asked, with a sneer. "Is that the only way you make money? You sit here and pick on people, upset their lives, use snipers to take out patsies, and then turn around and make even more people miserable?"

"If making people miserable was all I had to do, my life would be a walk in the park," the gunman muttered. "Listen. I don't give a shit either way. I just want what's on that key."

At his side, Amarylis shifted suddenly and asked. "It's got stuff about you on there, doesn't it?"

His face turned grim, as he pointed the gun right back at her face again.

She nodded. "That's the only reason anybody would be so adamant about getting it."

"You could be wrong there," he snapped, with a warning, an evident threat in his tone. "Guesses like that can get you killed."

"According to you, I'm apparently already in danger of getting shot anyway," she spat back in a bitter tone. "Do you know how many people have held guns on me lately? I came here to work on the dead, not to be a pawn for the living."

He snorted at that. "That's a pretty good line. Let me know how it works for you."

Amaryllis snorted. "It hasn't worked yet because assholes like you keep on coming." The gunman glared at her, and she shrugged. "Am I wrong? The body count is going up, and now, with that guard, you've hurt another person. If he dies, that's another one dead already, not to mention all the injuries." She shook her head. "That's just insane."

"Nothing is insane about it, but it's a good reminder that there's no life after this if we get caught. So we might as well just take out everybody we can." He gave her a knowing smile. "After all, … dead people don't talk."

"So you will shoot us right now?" she asked, her voice rising in shock. "Without the USB key? Just like that? It doesn't matter what we have planned for tomorrow or the next day? My life isn't worth anything to you? I'm just a piece of garbage to be taken out?"

"Yeah, that's pretty damn accurate, princess." He stared at her with amusement. "What world do you live in that you think anybody gives a shit about you? If they tell you differently, well, news flash, it's just all lies to make you feel better." He sneered. "That's the god-awful truth. The sooner you learn that, the better."

"And yet you're not giving me a chance to learn it," she noted bitterly, glaring at him. "All you're concerned about is shooting me."

"If you can get me the damn key, I'll keep you alive. However, you just said that you don't have any way to get the key."

"I don't," she repeated. "And I don't think the people who have the key want anything about it to become public knowledge."

"Ah"—he nodded—"now that makes more sense than anything you've told me so far."

"What does?" she asked curiously.

"About nobody wanting that to be public knowledge." He smirked. "Unfortunately that means you're quite likely telling the truth."

"Of course I'm telling the truth," she declared in outrage.

He snorted. "Most people lie. They'll tell you anything they think you want to hear, just to stay alive."

"Do you blame them?" she asked, looking at him askance. "People are just after a chance to live, to go on about their lives with some level of harmony. She glared at him. "Until you come along, and all you give a shit about is taking them out." She shook her head. "I don't get it. I've been dealing with the aftermath of all this death, but I don't get you guys taking people out in the first place."

He looked over at Tristan, with amusement on his face. "Does she not get it?"

"She wants to believe in Santa Claus still," Tristan replied. "She wants to believe in puppies and rainbows, all the good things in life."

"That's just bullshit," he said to her. "You'll learn very quickly that all of that is just a big lie."

"No, you don't get to choose," she argued. "You can

make it what you want it to be, but I make my own choices for me. You could also choose to make good choices instead of bad. Everything doesn't have to turn to crap."

At that, the gunman started to laugh and laugh. "Oh my God, she does believe it, doesn't she?"

Tristan nodded. "You could let her live. She's doing a good job here."

"What? Looking after the dead?" he asked, with a sneer toward her. "What the hell kind of work is that for a woman?"

She stiffened at that and glared at him. "What do you mean, it's not work for a woman? When you guys are done playing your little war games, who has to clean up the damn mess you all leave behind and find a way to restore some order?" She was fuming. "It's always the women who have to set things right, after assholes like you have flexed your egos twenty-four hours a day."

He glared at her and then laughed again. "You know, under different circumstances, I would probably like you."

"In different circumstances, I would still hate your guts because you're still trying to force me to do something against my will. You're still threatening my life. I have a life to live!"

"Why?" he asked, with a sneer. "You don't even have a partner."

She studied him. "So you know that, do you?" she asked calmly, eyeing him, her head tilted. "You have access to my personnel file?"

"Files are easy to get access to, and it sure as hell should be a whole lot easier."

"No, it shouldn't," she murmured. "We're supposed to have a secured system, so people can't get a hold of that stuff."

"Doesn't take much to blackmail somebody into giving you the information you need," he pointed out, "and, after they've done it once, you've got them for life. When I realized you guys picked up that evidence, I wanted to know everything about you."

"Good for you," Amarylis snapped.

"Yeah, and you didn't disappoint. Goody Two-Shoes all the way. It's also how I knew I could turn around and make you do what I wanted because you'll do anything, … everything to stay alive." He gave her a hard glint. "Women like you … always do."

"What do you mean, *women like me?*" she asked curiously.

"It's your nature."

"People do whatever they can to stay alive. We share this theory that, if you can survive, you might live and enjoy your life," she explained. "Only when assholes like you take everything away that they understand it's not so simple."

"So then I'm serving a good purpose here," he replied in a bored tone, as he looked around the small apartment and shook his head. "Look at this place. You even live like you're some pious being."

She stared around her apartment, and Tristan could see the confusion in her gaze. He didn't take his gaze off the gunman though—or off Jasper, who was slowly waking up and assessing the scenario. Tristan pointed out, "You and I both know that, if you can't get that key, … you're doomed, a dead man walking. So, for you, getting the key is everything."

"I'm glad you understand that, so you won't fight me about it."

"There is no point in targeting us," Tristan stated calmly. "We don't have it. We don't have access to it, and we cannot get it."

"That just means you're completely useless to me," he snarled, as he lifted his weapon.

A single shot was fired, and Amarylis cried out, as she threw herself into Tristan's arms. He held her close, holding her trembling body against his, as he whispered, "It's okay."

She stared up at him. "How can it be okay?" She looked around Tristan to see the gunman on the ground, still alive but cursing up a blue streak, with Jasper now on his feet, glaring down at him. Jasper had just shot her intruder in the shoulder.

"Asshole," Jasper muttered. "Did you think I would go down that easily?" Jasper asked their gunman.

"I should have shot you, you little fucker," he snapped.

"You should have, but you didn't," Jasper pointed out cheerfully, "and now guess what? … You're ours." And, with that, he slammed his fist into the gunman's face, knocking him out cold.

Tristan nodded at Jasper. "Nice job."

"Not me so much as her."

Tristan laughed. "She didn't even realize what she was doing."

She looked from one man to the other, clearly confused. "What was I doing?"

"Keeping our gunman busy," Tristan replied, "while Jasper got his wits about him."

"I didn't even realize you were okay," she admitted, staring at him. "How did I not see that?"

"I've got a hard head," Jasper shared, with a smiling yet pained expression. "Besides, when you take a blow like that, if you go with it, recovering is a whole lot easier."

She just shook her head, as she stared at him. "Did you just give me a lesson on how to handle being attacked?"

His smile was as gentle as possible, and he nodded. "You never know when you might need that little tidbit of information."

She swallowed and nodded, then added in a whisper, "How about just ... *never?*"

CHAPTER 8

Amarylis sat curled up in a corner of her own couch, sipping a hot cup of tea.

Tristan just recently got a call from Masters, saying he shot and killed what was probably the partner to her intruder. That didn't bother her so much right at this moment, except for the added tidbit of the scar down the right side of his face. She sighed. Once she got him in the morgue, she would check, but at present she pegged this latest dead guy for the same one chatting her up in her apartment parking lot earlier this week—or was it last week?

Anybody, any normal person, would say she was in shock. She kept talking herself out of it, but, to be honest, so many crazy things had happened over so many days now that she found it hard to imagine anything other than being in shock. She'd done better while she dealt with the bleeding of the gunman's wound, preparing him for the ambulance. However, once that was done, she sank into a muddled state again.

She gave herself a good headshake and muttered, "You're fine." Realizing she'd said it out loud, she winced and looked up to see both Jasper and Tristan studying her. "I'm fine," she repeated.

"And, if you keep saying that, you might convince yourself," Jasper noted.

She shrugged. "This isn't exactly normal in my world."

"It's not exactly the norm in ours either," Jasper pointed out, "but obviously we have a whole lot more experience at it than you."

"I'm not sure I even want to get that kind of experience either," she declared, giving him a wan smile. "Is your world always like this?"

Jasper just shrugged.

"No," Tristan replied, "usually our job isn't this dangerous. This Mason matter happens to be an exceptional case, which is also why we've been brought in."

She nodded at that. It made sense in a way, not that his job description was any clearer, but she understood that, for Tristan, he had drawn a fine distinction where these things were concerned.

Tristan walked over, sat down beside her, and took the teacup from her hands, placing it nearby on the coffee table. Then he pulled her into his arms and just held her.

She curled up deep into the warmth and the comfort he offered. She didn't say anything, and neither did he. He just held her. After a few minutes, she lifted her head and whispered, "Thank you."

He nodded. "It's not asking much to give yourself a break. This has been pretty traumatic for you."

"It has." She looked down where their prisoner was tied up. "Are there more foot soldiers coming after that damn key? Can the bad guys not keep their operations straight, or are they double-booking their crimes?"

"If two teams had been booked, the second one would already be here, so no. I don't expect a second team tonight.

That's one of the things we'll be quizzing him about here in a minute. That and a lot more."

"Why isn't the ambulance here by now?"

"We're not in any great hurry to get him any assistance. It's best if he's a little uncomfortable while we get some answers out of him."

"Is that what we have to do?"

"Have to? … No. Want to? … Damn right," he pointed out.

She winced.

"Look. This isn't how we prefer to handle it," he shared, "but we must get to the bottom of it. For whatever reason nobody wants to believe we don't have that key."

"Which was always the problem with it being taken away from us," she pointed out.

"Sure, for the first gunman maybe. What happens after the first guy came and got it? What would we tell the next one, or the one after that?"

She winced at that. "I was hoping they were all on the same team and communicating," she muttered.

"And they might be. We don't know. What I do know is that somebody here is involved in the sniper shooting of Mason and that several other people have been killed or injured because of this plot to kill Mason. Plus, we can't forget what they did to Nicholas."

At that mention, she remembered the poor investigator who'd been held captive and tortured for months. She straightened and glared over at their prisoner, still tied up. "Do you think he had anything to do with that?" she asked, feeling her own outrage rising to the forefront.

"I don't know, but the best thing is that he's alive, and that's one of the reasons we did what we did."

She frowned. "Did you expect Jasper to shoot him?"

"Well, yeah, it's what I would have done."

She snorted. "It's not what I would have done."

"Maybe not, but you would have done anything you needed to do to stay alive, no matter what that was, and we would all understand."

She groaned. "Let's hope I'm never put to the test because I'm not exactly sure what I would do. I did want to kill him at one point though. This scenario does render us down to absolute basic animal instincts, doesn't it?"

Jasper walked over and smiled down at her. "It absolutely does," he agreed, "but don't ever think that's wrong. At the core, our one basic need is to survive. That may sound selfish, but, for all intents and purposes, it's a good thing. Our survival skills and instincts come to the fore to save us. We do what we have to do to survive, and, through that, our species continues."

"Do you ever wonder if it should though?" she asked, frowning up at him. "Maybe we're just so far gone as a society that we shouldn't survive."

"It's occurred to me," he admitted. "I try not to think about it too often because, well, it doesn't bode well for humanity if I'm right. However, we do try hard to keep our perspective and to realize that, by helping the masses, you would like to think that the rest of us might survive as well."

"All throughout history we've done the most incredibly awful things to each other." Her voice almost broke as she spoke about this.

"Absolutely, but I would like to think that, even though we have unprecedented access to the news of all the horrific things happening in the world, maybe we are still one of the generations who's been easier on each other," Jasper shared.

"I get that probably sounds ludicrous to you, but I would like to think that we're improving."

"It's not ludicrous," she noted. "I'm just not sure it's realistic."

He grinned. "That's okay too, and I'm happy to try hard to believe that we're improving."

"Yet," she pointed out, "you have an injured prisoner tied up in my house."

He nodded, with a smile. "We do, don't we? Honestly, I'm absolutely thrilled about it."

She shook her head. "I'm not sure you should be quite so happy."

"Oh, I should be," Jasper countered, with a wolfish grin, "because just think. This is the first one we've got alive."

She looked over at the prisoner, who was glaring at her, as if he'd been listening all along. "Do you think he'll talk?"

The gunman snarled. "I have no intention of talking. I'm not even sure what the hell you did to me," he said, turning to look at Jasper. "Yet, when I get out of here, I'll make you pay for it."

"Oh, point taken, but you better act fast," Jasper replied, with a nod. "I highly doubt you will live more than one or two days though," he added, with a wave of his hand, "so I wouldn't worry about it."

The gunman just snorted. "You're one of the good guys, so you have rules to play by. I don't."

"The people you play with don't have rules either," Tristan pointed out, "and they've pretty much killed everybody else involved. So, it's not that we will kill you within a few days. Your side will take you out."

"No, they won't. They need me."

"Oh my God," Amarylis cried out, staring at him, "are

you so stupid? You are just the hired help. You can and will be replaced."

Tristan chuckled.

"That's what they all say," Jasper added.

The gunman glared at her. "What the hell?"

She nodded. "They've killed everybody, even guys just like you, who were right there in front of us, waving their guns around, saying they were needed too." She shook her head at him, glaring right back. "So cut your ego down to size and realize that these men don't give a crap if you live or die. … They have a temporary use for you, and that's it."

He shrugged. "You don't know anything about it."

"I know they end up on my table in the morgue. As far as I'm concerned, you will die too. I don't care if you end up on my case list. The prospect of cutting your bones apart doesn't exactly fill me with revulsion," she shared. "Got some heart disease in there? I'll find it. Broken bones from an abusive childhood? Don't worry. I'll see them. Anything you want to tell me about yourself before I take my knife to you?" she asked, her tone hard, as she glared at him. "There are no secrets once you're on my table." He appeared a little grossed out by her words.

"You seem to be such a nice person," he replied, with a sneer, "and then you talk like that, and everybody knows you're psychotic, waiting for the world to blow a gasket."

She laughed. "If I'm psychotic, what the hell are you?"

He smirked. "I'm somebody who makes shit happen in this world, but I don't expect you to understand."

She replied, "No, I sure don't, not with all this shit that's happening, all at the expense of others."

"You won't be making shit happen in a day or two more," Tristan pointed out.

The gunman rolled his eyes. "Christ, you're one of those little do-gooders too. No wonder you're hooked up with this one. You two deserve each other."

She nodded. "You're right. We do."

Tristan forewarned her, "You might not want to sit in on this next session."

She swallowed and nodded. "You're probably right." She stood and gathered her cup of tea and headed toward her bedroom. She stopped and pivoted to the gunman, saying some final words, "I'll see what they did to you when you're on my table anyway, but I sure as hell won't shed a tear." And, with that, she went into her bedroom and closed the door.

The gunman turned and looked at them, a sneer on his face. "Nice touch having your *softie* around." He laughed. "She doesn't know that you're limited by everything you're *not* allowed to do. I don't have that same limitation. So, when I get out of here, you're dead." He wore an odd expression, as he turned specifically to Tristan. "You have no idea what I will do to her."

"And, for that reason alone," Tristan stated, giving him a wry smile, "you'll never get to her."

TRISTAN HEARD THE door *click* as she went into the bedroom and knew that she'd heard that last line, and that was probably good. He didn't have anything to hide, and assholes like the one in front of him would not continue what they were doing, not with Tristan around. He looked over at Jasper and pointed at their captive. "All yours."

Jasper nodded. "So, what's on this key?" he asked the

gunman in a conversational tone.

The guy just glared at him and didn't say anything.

"I wonder if he's the gay lover," Jasper suggested, looking over at Tristan. "He looks gay, doesn't he?"

The guy stared at him in shock. "Good God," he muttered, "that's not what I look like." And then he laughed. "Not a bad opening salvo though."

"Not bad at all, is it? Particularly since we already know what's on the key." The other guy paled, as Jasper nodded. "So, it seems like you might have a vested interest in all of what's going on right now. Yet not a whole lot of people give a shit, not when we know that you're quite prepared to kill everybody in your orbit in order to save your own ass."

"You don't know anything," he snarled, "and I'm not on that key."

"Then somebody you care about is, or somebody else is on the list and is paying you enough that you're willing to be here," Jasper suggested, with a laugh.

"So maybe *his boss* is the gay lover," Tristan guessed, with a chuckle. "Maybe he's jealous. Maybe he'll take over his boss's spot, and he doesn't like competition."

The gunman just glared at him and didn't say anything.

"He does look gay though, doesn't he?" Jasper asked again.

"Yeah," Tristan agreed. "Definitely something about the way he's looking at you, … and the way he *wasn't* looking at Amarylis. I see what you mean."

"I don't like bitches," the gunman snarled.

"Exactly. We already figured that out," Jasper noted, as he and Tristan had a good laugh at the joke.

"I don't like bitches who psych me out," the gunman clarified, turning red. "It's got nothing to do with her."

"Then you don't understand what you're up against," Jasper declared, "because, whatever the hell is going on in your world, you're not getting out of this one."

A knock came on the door, and Jasper looked over at Tristan. He nodded, then walked to the door and waited until the MPs on the other side identified themselves.

When he opened the door and let them in, the gunman laughed. "See? You guys are all about following the rules."

"Not really," Tristan argued. "They're just here to haul you someplace where we don't have to worry about your screams and calls for help."

The gunman looked over at Jasper for help, and, for the first time, a shadow of fear crossed the gunman's face.

CHAPTER 9

Amarylis woke up, surprised to find that she must have fallen asleep at some point. She had fully expected to lay awake, knowing Jasper and Tristan were out there potentially torturing their prisoner. She tried to find sympathy in her heart for her intruder, but it was hard, damn it.

So many people had died already because of that stupid USB key. She almost wished she hadn't found it. Yet she knew that wouldn't have brought this blackmailing and the criminal acts to an end otherwise.

As she lay here in the bed, wondering how she could possibly have slept through a fist fight or whatever, a knock came on her bedroom door. She called out, "Come in," instinctively knowing that it would be Tristan. When he walked in, she smiled. "Hey." As he critically eyed her, she admitted, "Believe it or not, I fell asleep."

His eyebrows shot up, and then he nodded. "Considering the series of shocks you've been through, that's a good thing."

"Maybe, though I'm still stunned that all of this happened."

He smiled at her. "You're always so strong, but, at some point, everybody needs a break."

"Yeah? So, what about you? Have you slept yet?"

He shook his head. "I did want to tell you that the prisoner is no longer here."

She asked him, "Did you kill him?"

His eyebrows shot up, and then he grinned at her. "No, of course not. The MPs picked him up."

"Did you get anything out of him?"

"No, and we didn't expect to. So we will let him cool his heels in his cell awhile and think about it."

"Do you think it's safe for him?"

"We got him out of here safely," he shared, "and we're keeping him separated, so we're hoping so."

She nodded. "Maybe the reason you got him out of here safely is because he's the one who's been killing everybody else."

"That thought had occurred to us," Tristan acknowledged, with a nod of agreement. "We just don't know anything for certain yet, and we won't know for a while."

She winced at that. "I keep hoping that we'll get an end to this."

"And we will," he said, "maybe not as quickly as we want, but we are getting somewhere."

"Do you think he has something to do with what's on the key?"

"He told us it didn't have anything to do with him, and that may or may not be true. Still, it could be somebody he's protecting or is being paid by to retrieve it."

"But he's not talking."

"No, he's not talking," he confirmed.

"Damn, do you think he will?"

"I don't know. I'm hoping so. I'm going down there to have another chat with him."

"I'm just worried somebody'll kill him before you get any information."

"I think we're all worried about that," he admitted, with a shrug. "It's not something we can guarantee won't happen, but obviously we don't want it to. It seems like the only way to start getting some answers is to keep the pressure on him."

She nodded. "That sucks too."

"It does. It surely does." He hesitated, staring, not saying anything more.

She fidgeted under his scrutiny for a moment, then couldn't stand it anymore. "What?"

"I would like for you to take a few days off work."

She shook her head. "Oh no, not happening, don't even go there." He glared at her, and she smiled. "It won't happen, and no way would it happen if our roles were reversed and if you were being asked to do that."

"I told Jasper that you would be opposed to such an idea."

"Good, that means you're starting to get to know me."

"Yeah, I also knew you would be as stubborn as hell over it," he shared cheerfully.

"You're right. I am."

"And you will explain to him why you are being so stubborn?"

"I don't have to explain," she declared. "It's my job, and I came here in good faith. So I won't let them down over this."

"I don't think most people would consider this as letting anyone down, and I'm sure Dr. Cox wouldn't feel that way."

"Maybe not, but I also don't want to put more on him. He's already got it rough enough as it is."

"Does he?" He eyed her curiously.

"Yes, he does, and I'm not doing that to him."

He nodded. "I'll tell Jasper that."

"But you don't think he'll be happy about it, do you?"

"Nope, I sure don't," he agreed cheerfully, "but, as an adult, you get to make your own decisions. As somebody who cares what happens to you, it's not a decision I'm happy with, but I understand why you're making it and realize that you may be feeling oddly bereft. So I will head out now, but we're leaving an MP outside your apartment."

Her eyebrows shot up, and he nodded. "Remember how we expect more gunmen will come out of the woodwork, all for that damn USB. So this is not over yet."

"Oh, *great*," she muttered.

"Exactly. I'm glad you understand."

"You're leaving?" she asked cautiously.

"I am. I will go talk to your intruder, see if we can get him to open up a little bit."

"Do you think that's possible?"

"I don't know, but I have to try. A lot of other people's lives are on the line over this," he pointed out, looking at her, "and we don't want anybody else to die, whether they have something on that key or not."

"That's the thing, I guess. Everybody is protecting themselves, aren't they?"

"They are, even if nothing is criminally wrong on that USB key, still something is potentially career-ending."

"Yes, but to take someone's life over a lost career?" she asked, with a headshake. "That seems crazy."

He smiled. "I get that, for you, it probably sounds that way. Yet, for many of these people, this is their life, their world, and to have anybody ruin it for them is pretty big," he explained. "Maybe not big enough to warrant killing, but obviously others have a different opinion on that."

"It all sounds terrible," she stated, shaking her head. "To see people hurting others over it? ... I want to say it's unbelievable, but obviously it's not." She gave a dismissive wave of her hand. "I just think it's disgusting."

He grinned. "You and me both," he agreed cheerfully. "Now, I would very much appreciate it if you would check in with me, should you decide to go anywhere."

"I have to go to work," she noted, looking at him intently.

"I assumed as much," he murmured, "and the MP outside, he'll take you there."

She stared at him.

"Don't look at me like that," he said. "You know perfectly well that we're not out of trouble yet, so just say *thank you very much* and be happy with it."

She winced, but then did as he asked, quite literally to make the point. "*Thank you very much, and I'll be happy with it.*"

He burst out laughing, and she smirked at him. "At least that's the right attitude," he said, with a smile.

"Hey, some things are just a little easier than others," she murmured. "What time is it right now?" she asked, looking at her watch and struggling to read it.

"It's five. I heard you moving around in here, and it was time for me to get out of here anyway."

She groaned. "Five o'clock in the morning? I might as well just get up and go to work." He frowned at her, and she shrugged. "I do that sometimes."

"Not exactly a good habit to get into," he replied, raising an eyebrow.

"As if you wouldn't do the same," she scoffed.

Once again, he broke out into a free and open laughter. "Can't argue that. You're right about that for sure." She threw back the covers, and he asked, "Are you sure you don't want to get a little more sleep? It'll be a long day otherwise."

"It'll be a long day no matter what I do," she stated. "Let me get up, and I'll lock the front door behind you."

He nodded. "Fine." He walked out to the living room with her, and she had to admit it was such a relief to realize that no other men, military police or not, were in her living room. Tristan watched her reaction and grinned.

"Hey, you can't blame me," she muttered.

"Honestly, you've done so well that I'm sure everybody is pretty proud of you."

"Nobody should be proud of me," she declared, looking at him. "I didn't do anything."

"And yet what you did do was all good." He walked over to the door and looked back at her before opening it. "Keep the door locked. Keep yourself inside. Grab some more sleep if you can, and contact me when you go to work." Then he checked his phone, confirming the guard was in place outside her door. As he stepped out, he looked back at her.

She hated to say it but knew she looked like some woebegone orphan being left behind. He hesitated, and she waved him off. "I'll be fine."

"If you say it a few more times," he whispered, a gentle smile on his face, "you might believe yourself."

She shrugged. "I just have to get used to it."

He walked back over to her and took her in his arms. Tilting her chin up, he added, "Just remember that you aren't always alone." He gave her a gentle kiss, and, with that, he was gone, leaving her more bereft than ever.

When a knock came on her door shortly thereafter, she

almost thought it was Tristan again and opened it cautiously, only to see the MP standing in front of her.

He smiled and began, "Ma'am, my name is Scott. I just wanted to let you know that I'm here. Go back and get some sleep if you can." And, with that, he closed her door. She groaned. Everyone wanted her to go to bed, yet it was the last thing she wanted to do right now. She couldn't quite shake off the feeling that more trouble was ahead, and, even if she wasn't ready, somebody needed to be. She just didn't know who would be showing up today because this situation made no sense to her.

She did go back and lay down, trying to sleep but quickly gave up. After a shower, she put on some coffee. As she sat here in the early morning hours, waiting for dawn to arrive, sipping away on her coffee, her mind chewed through everything she knew about this mess so far.

It wasn't as if anything was clear-cut about it, nothing she could put a finger on, but it seemed past time for more answers, how something more should be unearthed along the way.

As she pondered the mess of the last few days, she couldn't imagine what these bad guys had gone through to try to get that USB key—even a copy might have made them happy. She didn't know for sure, but certainly some compromise could be made, maybe just paying some money to these hired killers to stop with their threats and to go hide out somewhere. People did all kinds of things for money that she didn't agree with and couldn't see the sense behind. Honestly, in her line of work, she'd seen men killed over five bucks.

She knew that it depended on the person and what was building up behind it. So something was on that key, but she hadn't necessarily seen very much. She'd noted some names in her emailed copy, as much of it as she had read, and she had a great memory. So she had certainly tucked away some of that information into the back of her brain. She hadn't bothered to share that information, but a certain level of self-preservation was involved here. Not that she would give this data to the bad guys. No way. They would just kill her after she told them. But the supposed good guys Tristan had handed over the USB key to? She had no way of knowing whether those higher-ups who had taken possession of the key were trustworthy or not.

As she sat here, she wondered if this last guy was connected to the other dead bad guys somehow, and whether Tristan had gotten the chance to even sort that out. It would likely take a little while, but something was almost familiar about him. She took a moment to replay some of the conversation in her mind, and then it hit her.

She got up, grabbed her phone, and quickly sent Tristan a text message. **My intruder hacked into my personnel files, yours too probably. Or he had a hacker do it for him. Plus, I think that guy from last night is related to the lady who knocked you out. He has a masculine version of her facial features.**

When her phone rang minutes later, Tristan greeted her, without preamble. "And here I thought you went to bed."

"I did try," she muttered almost apologetically, "but I just couldn't sleep."

He hesitated. "So you think Terry looks like her?"

"So his name is Terry? Good to know. And, yes, I do. However, when dealing with different genders, it's easy to miss the similarities."

"Give me a sec." He disappeared, and a few minutes later he came back on and added, "You could be right."

She laughed. "I *could* be," she quipped. "Just send in some DNA, and I'll confirm it." And, with that, she hung up, grabbed her outdoor gear and her bag, then knocked on the front door before she opened it. She told the guard, "I'm heading to work." When he frowned, she stated forcefully, "Yeah, and you can argue all you like, but I'm still going." He rolled his eyes, and she retorted, "Yeah, I get the same reaction from the others."

"I would guess you do," he noted. "Ma'am, you have to understand that everybody is just keeping you safe."

"They might be keeping me safe, but I'm also trying to solve this problem. So let's do both at the same time. Regardless, I damn well need to get to the heads and tails of this mess."

He frowned at her. "You seem to have something to go on."

"I certainly have a new lead, and I need to get to my office to work on it," she shared. "So either come with me or don't get in my way."

"You know my ass is on the line if I don't come with you."

"I'm sure it is," she agreed cheerfully. "Just make sure we get there safely. There's been enough shenanigans up until now."

"Right? Sounds like you've had a crazy few days."

"I have, and I'm more than done with it." She headed out to her car, and the MP raced up to the passenger side. "Don't you have wheels?" she asked him.

He shook his head. "Yes, but I'm going with you."

She rolled her eyes at that. "Fine, get in." She quickly let him in and drove to the morgue. As she parked, she turned to look at him. "Are you supposed to come inside or stay outside?"

"I'm supposed to stay with you," he replied. "Wherever you go, I go."

"I don't think you'll like this," she argued.

As they got upstairs and passed the forensics lab, he asked her carefully, "What do you do for a living?"

She looked over at him and laughed. "I'm one of the coroners here. I'm about to inspect some dead bodies." As she watched the color fade from his face, she burst out laughing. "That's all right. I don't have to drag you that far into my department."

"That's good," he muttered, "but I'm as game as the next guy. I just didn't expect that."

"Why? Don't I look like a doctor, somebody who deals with dead bodies?"

"No, ma'am, you sure as hell don't," he stated bluntly, "but then again you're with Tristan, and he's a bit different too."

"What do you mean, I'm with Tristan?" she asked, frowning at him. He flushed and didn't say anything more. She waved off his discomfort and added, "Don't worry about it. You're not treading on anything."

"I am because, if you're not acknowledging that something's between you," he noted cautiously, "then obviously I've stepped into the middle of something."

She laughed. "I wouldn't worry about it."

"You say that, but I don't want to get into trouble with you or with him." He gave her a bright smile as he admitted that.

"Good point," she acknowledged. "It makes sense that you're keeping everything close to your chest, but what's between me and Tristan is still fairly open-ended at the moment."

"Not for long," he muttered. "I've seen how he looks at you."

She smiled at him. "Thank you for that."

He nodded. "Not a problem. So, I don't have to go where the dead bodies are, do I?"

"No, you sure don't, unless you want to."

"No, I'm happy to skip that," he replied, with a mock shudder. When they got to the office, she quickly raced to her corner of the world. As soon as she got there, she turned and frowned.

He just frowned right back. "I'm going nowhere."

She rolled her eyes. "Yeah, I got that message."

"Good, so don't slip past me."

"Wasn't planning on it," she said, with a dismissive wave of her hand, "just not sure what I will do with you."

He shrugged. "How about you just ignore me?"

"I would love to. I really would." She pondered it and then shrugged. "I will be in there." And she pointed to her workroom.

He looked over and nodded. "I'll just stay right here."

"You do that," she said, with a smile.

With that, she quickly gowned up and headed into her workspace. There she pulled out the body of the woman they had found already murdered, and, while Amarylis worked, her phone buzzed. She answered it, distracted, only to hear Tristan's voice. "I'm sending over DNA."

"Okay, I'm pulling DNA off her right now, so I'll compare the two."

"So you think they're connected?"

"Yep, I sure do. I could be wrong, and I've certainly

been wrong before, but—"

"Yeah, well, you're likely to have the most experience in this anyway," he noted, with a complimentary tone.

"If you say so. But so what if they are related? All it does is give us a few more questions."

"We'll take anything we can get right now," he replied.

"Remember that my MP guard is here, so whoever is coming with my intruder's DNA had better be prepared to announce themselves."

"Yeah, so how's he handling that?"

"He's in my outer office," she stated in a dry tone, "not very impressed with the idea of coming with me into the morgue."

"I don't think I like the idea of him in your outer office either," he noted, his tone deepening.

"It's fine. We're locked up."

"Yeah, you say that, but now I have to send over a courier."

"Bring it yourself then," she suggested, "but I've got to get to work." And, with that, she ended the call. She quickly finished what she was doing, then started to run the DNA sample, wondering just what the hell was going on, and, if they were related, why would they be doing something like this? Was it for her, against her, or because of her somehow?

There were just so many avenues to pursue, and yet none of them gave them very much in terms of clear-cut answers. With that done, she turned and started taking photos of the woman from all angles, looking for something a lot more identifiable in terms of facial recognition. Tristan already knew who she was, but, if by any chance she was related to the gunman in her apartment last night, then Amarylis wanted to know too.

It wasn't long before she got another phone call from Tristan. "Now what?" she asked in exasperation.

Laughter filled his tone when he said, "I'm on my way up. I just didn't want to scare you."

"Oh, you're here already?" she asked, looking up and around.

"Yes, I am. Obviously, when you're here at work, I'm not a big part of your life."

"Whatever," she muttered. "I'm buzzing you through." She let him into the main part of the building and continued the call as she waited. When he sighed heavily, she asked, "What did you expect?"

"I need to see whether this relationship will work or not, and I guess I was just hoping that maybe, somewhere along the line, I would count as much as the lab."

"Presumably you're joking."

"I could be joking, but what does that mean to you?"

"Not a whole lot," she said cheerfully. "It tells me that you might …"

He walked into the lab just then, and she smiled. He walked over and handed her a tube, which she eagerly snatched from his hand, then headed to her machines and quickly set it up. "How long will it take?" he asked, recognizing that any other line of conversation was fruitless.

"Too long in some ways but likely a rush job about twenty-four hours at least," she said. "Comparing them of course, well, that's another step. However, it shouldn't take all that long either."

As a matter of fact, considering that she was well used to this equipment and the various machines, it still took long enough that she was standing here, impatiently waiting. She caught him grinning at her, and she smiled. "I get it, but it's something I can do, and I would like to know myself."

"I'm surprised you even saw it."

"I'm not. When visually comparing male to female, it's often much harder to see, but still siblings are often very close in appearance."

"They can be complete opposites too," he pointed out.

"Oh, absolutely. They can be, but, with any luck, that won't be the case today."

And, when the machine beeped, she walked over and studied the images for a moment, comparing the two DNA samples, with Tristan watching over her shoulder. She smiled. "So, if you compare these findings, what do you think?"

"They're identical, aren't they?"

"No, not identical, but they're definitely from the same mother," she clarified, pointing out the lines that matched. "So, we have a 99.6 percent possibility," she read from the report, "that they have the same mother."

"Interesting, so we have siblings."

"We do, and that is good news."

"It's good news but also bad news." He frowned, as he stared down at the machine.

"What's the bad news?" she asked, frowning now too.

"Just figuring out why and what."

"At least you now have another avenue to work with."

"We do, and I will go talk to Terry about that other avenue."

"You do that, and let me know."

"Let you know what?"

"What he says," she stated, looking at him.

"What do you expect him to say?" he asked, with a note of curiosity in his voice.

She smiled. "I suspect he'll lie through his teeth, though it's possible that he doesn't even know. They had different fathers, after all. So that's another avenue to pursue. However, the DNA doesn't lie."

And, with that, he nodded. "Thank you for this."

"Yep, no problem. Now get lost, so I can get back to my regular work."

But since she was laughing as she said that, he tossed her a big grin. "Dinner?" he asked. "And, yes, it's a date."

"Sure," she replied, as her heart sped up with joy. "Dinner sounds great, and maybe this time we can have a meal without any chaos."

"Oh, I wouldn't count on that," he declared, with a big grin on his face. "But it's nice to know you're somebody who can handle it, even if it happens."

And, with that praise, he was quickly gone, but he left her with a smile on her face and a sense of accomplishment for at least achieving something in this mess.

TRISTAN HEADED BACK to the holding cell within their own department, where they kept the gunman off the grid, so to speak. As Tristan walked in, he began, "So, Terry." The man didn't shift either way, just giving Tristan a bored expression. "I'm wondering if you're involved because of your sister, or was she involved because of you?"

Only the slightest eye movement belied anything, but it was enough.

Smiling, Tristan nodded. "Now that we know that, I can inform you that your sister is lying in the morgue ..."

At that, Terry's eyes widened. "What?"

"Did you not know?" he asked. "How is that possible?"

The man wore a frantic expression. "No, no, no, no. What are you talking about?" He leaned forward, a sense of urgency in his tone, as he asked, "What are you talking about?"

Tristan opened his phone and snagged a couple photos he had of the dead woman in the morgue and flashed his phone at the gunman.

Staring at it in disbelief, he looked up at Tristan. "This isn't possible."

"Why is it not possible?"

"It can't be," he said. "It just can't be."

Shrugging, Tristan replied, "It is true. Her body's at the morgue right now."

"No, it's just a fake photograph."

"You want to see more photos?" he asked patiently. "I can phone our friend at the morgue for some real-time candid shots."

At that, Terry's face twisted. "I don't trust that one anyway. This is impossible. No way she's dead."

"Why is that?"

"She's too smart," he said, with an offhand look. "Just no way she's dead."

But a distinct note of fear in his tone made Tristan realize just how worried he was. "What does it change if she is dead? I'm texting and asking for a few more photographs, since you don't believe me, but what does this change in your world?"

"What do you mean, what does it change?" he asked, staring at him. "It changes … freaking … everything."

"Tell me more," Tristan said. When his phone beeped, he brought up one more photo and held it out, then quickly swiped through several more. The gunman's face went from bright red in fury to pure white, as the realization settled in that it was true. He closed his eyes and whispered, "Dear God."

"Now do you want to tell me what the hell difference it makes?"

He opened his gaze, but the look in his eyes wasn't nice, wasn't friendly, and, if anything, it promised murder.

Tristan stared right back. "I didn't kill her. Your boss man hired a local hit man to kill her for making a mistake on her job."

"I don't know what your problem is," Terry grumbled, leaving it at that, as if making a point.

"We've got our own problems to solve here and no shortage of other dead bodies too," Tristan added, "so do you want to talk to me about your sister or not?"

Terry shook his head. "She shouldn't even be in the mind of the likes of you," he muttered, his fury evident by the expression on his face. "She's good people."

"She *was* good people," Jasper interjected, walking up behind Tristan. "Have you forgotten the photos? She's dead. Somebody popped her, and we're pretty sure it was someone assigned to cleanup duty."

Terry's gaze widened, and he shook his head. "No reason for them to do that."

"Yet they seem to think they had good reason, and they have had several other people killed as well," Tristan shared. "Everybody we've had a chance to speak with in this mess has the same opinion, that none of it could possibly go wrong right before they were shot execution style. You people are all too naïve. Everyone thinks that a bullet ordered from your boss man couldn't possibly have anything to do with them. Yet here we are, with your sister dead, with you here in jail, in trouble for your little armed intruder and possible kidnapping stunt, amid an ever-growing number of bodies."

"What bodies?" he asked suddenly.

Jasper looked over at Tristan, who nodded, then pulled up his phone and quickly swiped through pictures of Drew. He held up Drew's face. "Recognize this one?" he asked, as Terry went silent. Tristan nodded, then swiped to the gunman he popped in the hospital, now residing in the morgue. "Or this one?" He watched as Terry's face paled in reaction.

He whispered, "Dear God, no."

"Unfortunately it's a *dear God, yes* moment, so I don't know what you think will protect you in all of this. However, I can tell you right now that it doesn't look like anything will protect you."

Amarylis's armed intruder sat here, almost stunned for several long moments, and then he announced, "I want protection."

Tristan shared a look with Jasper.

Jasper turned to Terry and shrugged. "Protection is one thing, but these guys are shooting everybody on sight," he stated. "They already know that you've been picked up."

He nodded. "They'll know, and they already have somebody out there to take me out. Why are you even holding me? I didn't do anything."

"But you did," Tristan argued. "You entered somebody's apartment without her permission and terrorized her with a gun."

"You knocked me out cold too. Don't forget that," Jasper noted from the sidelines.

At that, the gunman's lips curled. "That's nothing, and you know it. I could get off with a walk in the park."

"Maybe, but not when your actions are connected to so many other murders."

He paled and shrugged. "I didn't have anything to do with any of that."

"And yet we can prove that you and your sister were *both* connected to these murders," Tristan declared. "So that doesn't wash either."

The gunman glared at him. "I didn't have anything to do with her part in this," he said in the same wearisome tone, yet tinged with a hint of fury.

"You keep saying that. Yet here you are in our custody because of your own crimes, and you're not even talking about your sister's crimes."

"My sister was a good person, and she should never have been hurt because of this."

"Now the question is, did she get you involved, or did you get her involved?" He pinched his lips together, and, at that, Tristan nodded. "Poor woman, she didn't have a clue what she was in for, did she?"

Terry stared but didn't say a word.

Tristan was pretty fed up as he looked over at Terry. "Every criminal thinks it will be a walk in the park, like they'll get there, get in, do whatever shit they get to pull, and then they'll get to walk on out and totally get away with it all."

"Yet it's not like that at all," Jasper noted. "I don't know who in their right mind thinks they'll walk in and walk out on these unlawful jobs, but it hasn't happened yet, and it won't."

"You don't know that." Terry snarled at him. "Nobody

was supposed to get hurt."

"You believed that?" Tristan scoffed.

"What about Nicholas? Did you have anything to do with him?" Jasper asked.

The gunman frowned at Jasper. "What are you talking about?"

"Nicholas, remember?" Jasper repeated, looking over at Tristan, who now brought up Nicholas's photo. He held it up, and the gunman shrugged.

"I don't know that one."

"You've never seen him before?"

"No, I sure haven't."

"Did you ever hear about them holding someone?"

He shook his head again. "No, you can't pin that on me."

"I can pin all kinds of shit on you," Jasper declared, with a smile, cheerful as always. "Including the fact that you're connected to most of these deadly incidents. So, whether it's a direct connection or not, it won't matter to the judge and the jury, a military jury at that, … and you know it. The chances of your getting out of this are slim to none," Jasper noted, with a wave of his hand. "The only way I can see you getting out is with a bullet between your eyes, just like every other person you're involved with."

The gunman paled and didn't say anything.

"Now that you know your odds, you asked for protection. What is it you've got to give in return?" Jasper asked.

"Protection first," Terry snapped. "Then I'll talk."

"You say that, but I don't know that you have any goods to be bothered with."

"Yes, you do, and you know exactly what I'm talking about."

"No, I don't, and you need to tell me. If you want protection, I have to go to somebody who can arrange it, and they won't do it on a whim. As a matter of fact, after all the shit you and the people around you have pulled, chances of getting anything for you are slim to none."

"Then why am I even talking to you?" Terry snarled. "Just leave me alone."

"I can—hell, they can probably even get to you in here, considering how many guys have been taken out already."

"They *can* get us in here," Terry confirmed, followed by a sigh. "Maybe that's all there is to it. Maybe I'll just be taken out, like the others."

Tristan frowned, but he knew what was coming next. "Somebody in here is involved, aren't they?"

The gunman spat out just one word, "Protection."

Tristan looked at Jasper and said, "Over to you."

Jasper nodded. "I can talk to them, but, without any concrete benefit, they won't call me back." As he walked to the door, he turned to look back at Terry. "Don't waste my time because, if you haven't got anything to save your sorry hide, it'll just piss them off."

"Ooh, look. … I'm so scared," he snarled.

"Oh, you're scared," Jasper noted calmly. "You just don't want to admit it. Remember this. If your boss man gets to you before we have your protection in place, then your sister died in vain. You didn't get any retribution or revenge for the boss man killing off your own sister, before your boss man kills you off too." And, with that, Jasper turned and walked out.

Tristan followed, leaving Terry all alone.

CHAPTER 10

W^{HEN} A^{MARYLIS} G^{OT} a phone call toward the end of the day, she just knew it would be Tristan. She groaned as she answered it. "Are you canceling our dinner date?"

After a moment of surprise, he replied, "I guess it wouldn't be good if I did, *huh?*"

"If you have a good reason, then, of course, you do what you've got to do, but I was looking forward to it."

"Good," he said, "because I wasn't calling to cancel."

Smiling, she asked, "What's the problem then?"

"I just wanted to ask if I could meet you at the restaurant, as I'm held up here for a bit."

"Sure, we can do that. What time?"

"How about six? But make sure you take your guard with you."

"Sure, it's not as if he's had an easy day of it, as I've been on the tables most of the time. The poor guy had it much worse than he expected," she shared. "I had a lot of them today, but nothing quite so bad as what you've been dealing with though."

"And yet your information brought about a breakthrough, so we appreciate that."

"Good, I'm glad I could be useful. You can fill me in at dinner." And, with that, she laughed and was gone.

He sent her a thumbs-up and a heart emoji in a text right away, almost making her feel bad for hanging up but not quite. As she got through the rest of her day, she went to find her guard. "So, apparently you're still on duty, *huh?*"

"Apparently so," Scott said, with a nod.

"You don't have anybody to switch out with you?"

"I'll switch out when it's time to switch out," he shared, with a gentle smile. "Don't you go worrying about me." She frowned at him. He grinned back at her. "Besides, you should be getting away from all that nastiness in there soon, right?"

"Maybe," she said, with a smirk, "but it's a nastiness I'm used to."

"How is it that you can even think about doing that stuff?" he asked, with a shudder.

"It doesn't require thinking at all. It's what I'm good at, what I trained for, and it doesn't bother me at all."

"That's the part I don't get," he replied, staring at her. "You look so sweet and innocent, and now here you are, carving up bodies all day."

At his description, she laughed. "I guess for some people that sounds very strange, doesn't it?"

"Uh, yeah, like for everybody. I can't imagine there is anything *not* disturbing about it for most people."

"That's because most people don't want to think about death, but it's a natural part of living. The one guarantee you have when you're born is that you will die. You just don't know when or how."

"I prefer it that way myself," he muttered.

"Maybe, but a lot of people do want to know," she

pointed out. "We can't always give them that level of information. Sometimes I don't think we should either."

"Why is that?"

"Because I think we would probably live better if we didn't know when that day was happening."

He shrugged. "If we did know the day of our death, in some ways we might appreciate every day a little bit more and make the most of it."

"Maybe," she agreed. "Anyway, it's time to meet Tristan at the restaurant."

"*Right*." He chuckled. "From the morgue to a date."

She rolled her eyes. "Still not sure about how this whole date thing came about."

"That's easy," he replied, with a grin. "It's when a man meets a woman, and they fall in love."

She burst out laughing, which she knew was exactly what he intended, but he had said it in such a comical way that it was hard not to.

"Glad you've got a sense of humor," he replied, with that smile of his.

"Yeah, I do, and sometimes it's the only thing that keeps me going."

"You do deal with all those creepy things on the table over there."

She nodded in amusement. "Most people wouldn't say bodies were creepy."

"They obviously don't spend enough time with you then," he quipped. "My God, the things you do to them."

"Yes, and all in the name of science and getting answers for people," she explained.

"I get it. I do, but I don't think I would ever want my body autopsied. You're not kidding when you say you get into every bit of their life."

"That's because I have to, in order to get the answers. So, we have to cut open all parts of the body and see what's going on," she clarified. "And, once we've made as many cuts as we need to, if the answer is still not there, then we have to dig deeper, and sometimes we have to go even farther. But still, generally the body gives up its answers—not always, not every time. However, if we're lucky, the body does release those answers and makes our lives just a little bit easier."

He shook his head at that. "I still think it's creepy."

She laughed. "That's fine. You keep thinking it's creepy." She waved him off. "I'll keep doing my job regardless."

With a mutual agreement to stay out of each other's work, she headed home where she quickly had a shower and got changed. When she stepped out again, her guard, Scott, nodded approvingly. "You clean up nice, Doc."

She batted her eyes at him. "Gee, thanks, damned with faint praise."

He flushed. "I didn't mean it that way," he said awkwardly.

"Oh no, that's okay. I always put away my knives before I go out on a date."

"Good, I can't imagine dating somebody who was touching dead bodies all day."

"The thing is, I leave the bodies in the morgue," she noted. "It's not something I work on at home. Just think of all the guys who bring their work home, and be happy that I don't."

He stared at her in shock and asked, "The coroners couldn't do that though, right?"

"No, they sure couldn't," she reassured him, and then

she shrugged. "Sometimes we have to bring tissue samples and things like that home." He shuddered and she laughed. "They would be under microscope glass, so it's not that big of a deal."

"Yeah, you say that," he muttered, with a mocking grin. "So Tristan told me to drive you to the restaurant and that he would bring you home," he shared, with a waggle of his eyebrows.

"Good," she replied calmly, "that suits me just fine. That way I can have a drink and not worry about driving."

"Right, *drinking*. So I guess I could be driving you both home then, *huh?* Still, he did warn me that he might get called off of your date, so I should stick around, just in case."

"Our date could be interrupted with a call from his team," she noted. "As far as drinking goes, I don't think Tristan ever allows himself to unwind enough to have anybody else drive him."

"I think you may be right." Scott frowned. "Those guys, they have a hell of a reputation."

"I would imagine it's more than a reputation," she noted, "or at least a reputation that they earned fairly."

"Oh absolutely," Scott agreed, with a nod. "They're still scary dudes though. They have that reputation, and it's definitely something that we respect, but it's also something that we hold slightly apart from the rest, just because we know they're the people they are."

"And yet good people," she said uncertainly.

"Oh, you don't have to convince me."

"I was hoping you would convince me."

"Ah, … well, I've been watching some of that team for a long time," he shared. "I often wondered about becoming an investigator myself, but, if it means going into your morgue on a regular basis"—he held up his hands—"no thank you."

She grinned at him. "Just think, by then you could be totally comfortable in my morgue."

"I doubt it. I don't think anybody could be comfortable in there."

"And yet you forget that I don't work alone. I have assistants, technicians, and Dr. Cox, my boss, who works there with me. Also we have admin people, and then all kinds of work that people clean up after us."

"Oh no, no, no, hell no."

That image may have been too much for Scott. She burst out laughing as they walked outside and got into the MP's car. When he turned it on and pulled out of the parking lot, she asked, "Did Tristan tell you where we're going?"

He nodded. "Yeah, he sure did."

"Good, because I don't know all that many places around here yet."

"We have a lot of places to get a good meal here," he noted, with a smile, "and Tristan seemed pretty adamant that you will like this one."

"Good. I trust him, so whatever he picks out is just fine with me," She yawned, rubbing at her face.

Scott frowned. "You shouldn't have gone into work today. You're tired."

"I am tired, but it's a good tired. It's a tired borne of doing something good, of helping out. You know, that kind of tired."

"Maybe so, but still you work too hard."

"You're not the first person to tell me that," she admitted, with a chuckle, "and you won't be the last, so thank you, but I'm fine."

"In other words, butt out, right?" he asked, with a note of humor.

"Sure, *butt out* works."

At the restaurant, Scott parked, checking out their surroundings, and said, "Come on. Let's go." And he walked her inside.

When she saw Tristan, she felt relief easing the tension inside her and gave a long sigh.

Scott chuckled. "See? I told you that he would be here, the lucky sod." She shrugged. "Hey, outside of your job, you're pretty hot," Scott shared, and, with that, he stepped back out of the restaurant.

Surprised at his comment, she shook her head and walked over toward Tristan, who was standing up, waiting for her.

"Hey," he greeted her, as she arrived at the table. "I hope you're okay that Scott brought you here?"

"It was fine. I have to admit that I was a little perturbed because I wasn't sure if everything was okay out there. You get a little spoiled having personal treatment like this."

He smiled at her. "It's okay, and Scott is nice."

"I'm glad to hear that. I would hate for him to be one of the bad guys."

Tristan winced at that. "We all would, and we definitely know somebody in our world is double-crossing us," he shared, "but we haven't figured out who just yet."

She winced and nodded. "So, in other words, still watch my back."

"Always, but I wouldn't have had you with Scott if I didn't trust him."

"Sure, but it seems as if these days we don't know who we can trust," she muttered. She sat down in the chair that he held for her, and as soon as she was seated, he walked back around and sat down across from her. She smiled. "You look a little tired."

"A little tired is definitely something I can deal with. I didn't get a whole lot of sleep last night."

She nodded. "I was wondering about that. Just because I went back to sleep for a little while doesn't mean you got that opportunity."

"Nope, I sure didn't," he confirmed, leaning closer to her, "but our prisoner is still alive, so we'll take that as a good thing."

"I hope he stays that way," she replied in a serious tone. "In all honesty, I do. There's been so much death already."

Tristan nodded. "That's definitely something we're concerned about, and we do have security on him, but it's only as secure as we can make it."

She nodded. "And I suppose you carefully chose his guard."

He smiled. "The ones who we have looking after Terry have been thoroughly vetted, so that's not a concern."

"Glad to hear that, so …" She looked around to see if a waitress was coming.

"You're hungry?"

"I am," she admitted, with a smile, "so if food is available, bring it on."

"Food is always available." He chuckled.

Just then the waitress arrived, bringing two glasses of red wine. Amarylis smiled in delight as one was placed in front of her and the other with Tristan. "Look at that, a man who likes to make decisions."

He raised an eyebrow.

"I've met a lot of guys who would never order a glass of

wine for a lady," she shared, with a smile, "just in case it was wrong."

"If it was wrong, it could be easily changed," he noted. "Besides, that doesn't mean I wouldn't take care of the extra glass too."

She chuckled. "It always seemed to me that it would be an easy thing to do, and I do enjoy a good glass of wine and a red one at that, so that's an interesting choice."

"It's just how I like it and hoped you would appreciate some too."

Amarylis hadn't even had a chance to look at the menu, feeling too tired to even deal with it. More as a challenge to him than anything, she asked, "What are you having?"

"A steak with a baked potato and a Caesar salad."

Smiling, she said, "That sounds great. Make that two."

He nodded, and the waitress returned, so he quickly ordered, including toppings for the potato. "Was that a bit of a challenge or just you tired?" he asked Amarylis.

"Both," she said, followed by a yawn. "I'm tired. The lack of sleep has definitely affected me."

"Of course, but we'll get you a good meal, hopefully in a relaxing atmosphere, so then you can go home and get some sleep."

"That's the hope, but I don't know if it will work out that way."

"Let's hope so. We do have the one prisoner still, and he's formally asked for protection."

She stared at him, her jaw slowly closing in shock. "Seriously?"

He nodded, a grin on his face. "Jasper's working on arranging it right now. I've been waiting all afternoon and was finally relieved of guard duty when Masters came in, so I headed out."

"Interesting that our intruder has changed his tune on that," she noted, staring at him.

"Every once in a while, we do catch a break."

"But he hasn't told you anything, has he?"

"No, not until we make an agreement with him," he said, with an eye roll.

"I guess you can't blame the guy."

"Maybe not, but, once Terry realized his sister was dead, which did take a bit for him to believe, he looked at things differently. I also think he recognized Drew, Mason's sniper, though Terry didn't say anything, but his facial expression did. He didn't appear to know anything about Nicholas."

"And that's the other investigator who was missing for so long, right?"

He nodded. "Exactly."

"Interesting," she murmured. "How much of this is multiple arms of the same headache?"

"Anything is possible," Tristan noted cheerfully. "It'll be hard to know, until we get further down this pathway. However, we are pretty excited about potentially having somebody to talk to and to get more information from."

"And Masters is okay? You trust him?"

"Absolutely. Master's is one of the good guys."

"It seems all the good guys work in your department," she said, with a smile.

"Some of them are our own hand-picked guys, and we totally trust them. Hard to keep the good guys down," he added, with a smile.

She sighed. "But, if something does go wrong, you will lose yet another witness."

"Don't say that. That's not what we want to hear."

"Of course not. I'm sorry. I didn't mean it that way."

"No, it's all right. We're certainly aware that this is a problem, but we're hoping that it isn't *that* big of a problem."

She just nodded and didn't say anything.

A few minutes later Tristan's phone buzzed, and he winced and apologized. "Sorry, but I do have to take any calls coming in."

"Take them, and keep me filled in."

He laughed, looked down at his phone. "It's Jasper." In a low voice he answered the call, and she heard just a little bit of the conversation. When he hung up, he was smiling. "Good news. Sounds like your intruder made a deal."

"That is great news. So, what will you do after dinner?"

"I was hoping to get some sleep, but instead I'll head back to see what we can get out of this guy."

"Oh, wow. Even tonight?"

"Yes, especially tonight. We can't give the bad guys too much time to find Terry."

She winced and nodded. "You're right. I guess I was thinking that, at some point in time, you would get off this godforsaken case."

"At some point in time I will," he declared, with a smile, "but not today." She nodded. "Does that bother you?" he asked after a moment.

"Does what bother me?"

"The hours I work."

Surprised, she shook her head. "No. Do the hours I work bother you?"

"Sure," he admitted cheerfully, "I might give you a talking to because you work too much. Then I may chew you out for not taking more time off."

"Ah, and will you take more time off?"

"No, and you probably won't listen to me either."

"Nope, I wouldn't. Yet I do think, in that regard, we will both understand each other."

He looked over at her and smiled. "I'm pretty sure that's a given." As they talked about various things going on in their worlds, she asked him, "After you solve the Mason matter, will you be staying here on base and working in this investigation department?"

"Possibly," he said, with a thoughtful look. "I haven't been offered a full-time job yet, but I've certainly been offered a job with him. Jasper has taken over the department, although that's not public news yet."

"That's good though, right?" she asked him.

"It is, but I also don't know how many of the other guys on the initial investigation team will stay or will have the option of staying, and that in itself has caused some hard feelings."

"And yet that's not your problem."

He burst out laughing and nodded. "You're right. It isn't, and yet somehow … it is."

"Right. Things have a way of becoming our issues just because of who we are."

"Exactly." Their steaks arrived soon afterward, and that ended up being one of the best meals she'd had in a very long time.

When they were finished, she patted her stomach. "Gosh, I can't remember the last time I ate that much."

"You did fair justice to it," he noted in admiration as he eyed her almost-empty plate.

She pointed to his and added, "Not quite as good as yours though."

"Ah, I was very hungry."

"Obviously," she muttered. When his phone rang again, she held up her hands. "Sounds like our signal for dinner to be over."

"It could be." He checked the text and muttered, "I'm sorry."

"Don't be sorry. There will plenty of times when I'll have to step away because of work too."

He looked over at her and smiled. "Sounds like you think we should continue this relationship."

"Oh, I do. It's lovely to find somebody who's as much of a workaholic as I am."

He rolled his eyes at that. "I can see how you might think that, but I'm pretty sure we're supposed to help each other to do less of it."

"That will remain to be seen," she noted, with a chuckle, "but the good news is that, even in this crazy turbulent time, it appears we have found each other."

"I agree because that's exactly how I feel."

She nodded. "In that case"—she tilted her head and gave him a smile—"let me get home and get some sleep. Then we'll talk tomorrow. Of course, if you figure out anything you can share, I would love to hear it," she added.

"If I can share, I will, and that's always the challenge," he admitted.

"But I do this work too," she noted, "so I get it, and I would never ask you for anything more than you can give." The smile on his face warmed her heart.

Tristan walked her outside, noting Scott was waiting by his car. Looking up at Tristan, Amarylis suggested, "We could give Scott a bit of a show."

Tristan burst out laughing and pulled her into his arms.

"I'm not too worried about giving Scott a show, but, damn, I would love a good night kiss." He pulled her into his arms and kissed her with a ferocity that surprised them both. When he pulled back, he whispered, "Wow, I didn't mean for it to come across quite like that."

"Oh, don't say that," she murmured, "because I wanted it to come across exactly like that."

His eyes widened, and a twinkle entered his gaze. "Does that mean I'm supposed to come to your place after work?"

She pondered that and said, "If I didn't think it would likely be two o'clock in the morning, I might take you up on it, but how about another night?" She tapped his bottom lip. "Hold on to that ferocity, will you?"

"Absolutely," he murmured, as he leaned over and kissed her again. "Now let's get you home and into bed." He walked her over to Scott's vehicle, keeping a watchful eye out the whole way.

Taking his orders to heart, she got into the car with Scott and waved at Tristan until they were out of sight.

Scott muttered, "Okay, you're both some years older than I am, but, damn, even I could tell that was laying it on pretty heavy."

She chuckled. "It might have seemed like laying it on pretty heavy to you, but, honest to God for us, it was wonderful."

"It did look that way too," he admitted. "It made me feel envious for a moment."

"Don't you have a girl?"

"Nope, not at the moment. She didn't like the hours I work."

"That was part of the discussion we just had." Amarylis chuckled. "The fact that we're both workaholics may work for us."

"From what I've seen, you both are workaholics, but it seems you suit each other."

"Good, that kind of talk is never wrong."

"Says you," he muttered, with an eye roll, "but seeing the two of you makes me think it would be nice to meet somebody again."

"It would be," she agreed. "I've been alone for a long time, just waiting, seeing what was right in my world."

"Do you think Tristan's right for your world?"

"I do," she stated, with a smile. "I do."

"I hope you're right," Scott replied, "because, man, the two of you and that kiss? That was enough to make me want to go find a girl right now." She burst out laughing, and he grinned at her. "Hey, at least I'm honest," he protested.

"At least you're honest," she agreed, still chuckling. "Just pick the right woman for you. Now get me home so I can get some sleep, then wait for a chance to see Tristan again."

"Won't you see him tomorrow?"

"Oh, I'll see him tomorrow," she said, with a silly grin.

"Or tonight?" he asked, with a knowing smile.

"No, not tonight. We both decided sleep was a necessary thing, and he may not be off work for several more hours yet."

"Right," Scott murmured. "It's always about sleep, isn't it?"

"Sometimes it is, but sometimes it's about grabbing the moment because the moment's there. Other times it's literally just about enjoying what time you have because you never know when it'll be gone."

"Ouch, and that's you talking about the morgue again."

She burst out laughing. "My job may color my thinking,

but I've also seen a lot of life, and I want to see a whole lot more yet," she pointed out.

"Good," he agreed, as he pulled up to her apartment. "Now let's get you upstairs so you can get some sleep and be all sparkling and fresh for your boyfriend tomorrow."

She chuckled. "I don't know about *boyfriend.*"

"Oh, don't worry. We've all already heard that you are off limits." When she raised her eyebrows, he shrugged. "Tristan made it fairly clear right off the bat that you were his."

"I can't say that I appreciate that highhanded possessive BS," she conceded, frowning at Scott, "but considering Tristan's keeping me safe, I won't argue the point right now either."

Scott laughed. "Somehow I don't think you're all that upset about him warning off the rest of us, especially considering he's looking after you and is clearly smitten."

"If you say so," she muttered uncertainly, shaking her head.

"Oh, I do." He saw her expression and laughed. "It's all good."

LEAVING AMARYLIS WAS one of the hardest things Tristan had ever done. As far as timing went, it was shitty, except he didn't just want some quick roll in the hay. He was all about taking time to enjoy the moments that they had, not just get in and out, pardon the pun. He smiled at his own joke, knowing that it wasn't very funny, considering the stage of life they were both at. He wanted to take her away and spend a week together, just the two of them, getting to know each other apart from all the stress and panic they were both dealing with. That way they could find out who they both were on the inside and how compatible they would be.

He had a pretty good idea, but it wasn't the same thing as walking on the beach and holding hands, talking until the midnight sun disappeared, or smiling when you wake up beside her because she's still there, still part of your heart.

He wanted to show her so many things and take her around the world to see more. He didn't have a clue if she liked traveling, and that could be an issue because it was important to him. He liked getting out and acknowledging how much of the rest of the world was available, just waiting to be explored. This was something that he loved to do and so hoped they would have a chance to explore together.

He headed back to the office, exhausted, knowing he would have to take a break somewhere along the line. As he popped in, the place was empty. Frowning, he looked around, then headed for the couch in his office. He would give himself just a few minutes until the others showed up; sleep had been in short supply lately, and he was starting to run on empty.

He closed his eyes, and, before long, something jarred him out of sleep. He quietly remained on the couch, wondering what woke him. Then he heard voices, thought to sit up, but something prodded him to stay silent in the darkness.

"It's got to be in here, Lem," somebody growled. "Somewhere."

"I don't know whether it's in here or not," Lem snapped. "All we know is that it's no longer at the scene."

"We also know that it was picked up and bagged with evidence, that it disappeared from the lockup at the lab, and that somebody wants it forever."

"Of course they do," Lem snarled. "So we have to be in and out of here fast. We can't get caught inside, Stu."

"Fast or not," Stu snapped, "we aren't leaving until we have it."

Shifting to the floor, Tristan rolled over until he was tucked up against the desk, knowing that eventually they would come into this room.

"We've got a damn-short window to find that thing, and then we have to get out of here."

"How long do you think we have?"

"He told me not more than twenty minutes."

"Shit, that won't be long enough. This building is huge."

"It has to be."

Shaking his head at that, Tristan texted Jasper and then Masters. He didn't know where the hell everybody was or if something had gone wrong and had nixed their meeting. He expected some of his team would be here already, but they weren't and right now he could use some backup.

He heard the two voices, *Lem and Stu*, and, if only two were here, Tristan could get out of this just fine, even without backup. However, he didn't want these assholes to leave. He knew the desired USB key wasn't here, but would these two listen to him telling them that fact, if they found him? Probably not, not any more than the others had so far.

With his own weapon out and beside him, he waited to see if they entered his room. He heard chaos in the room outside, as they searched through as many desk drawers as they could. Yet, if they didn't even know what the USB key looked like, it would be almost impossible for them to find anyway.

Maybe that was intentional. Maybe somebody had deliberately *not* told them what to look for or had *not* shared how unique this particular USB was.

Then one of the men muttered in frustration, "What does it even look like, for Christ's sake?"

"I already told you. He mentioned it was unique, shaped like some car."

"A car?" he repeated, with a sneer. "Are you sure he's not just losing it?"

"Doesn't matter if he is or not. He's paying us. Remember that."

They quickly raced from one room to another, one desk to another, and when they finally stepped into the room Tristan was hiding in, he hunkered deeper inside the well under the desk, where the chair went. When the chair was abruptly pulled out, a man sat down and started opening drawers. Tristan just waited with his eyebrows raised, but they didn't even once look underneath. Of course the room was still in darkness, as they used flashlights to search through things.

"I don't see anything, Lem," the man in front of Tristan growled. He pushed the last desk drawer closed and stood up, kicking the chair farther back.

"Hey, nobody is supposed to know we were in here," his partner Lem added. "Remember that."

"Too damn late for that," Stu grumbled. "I've left a trail everywhere." After a moment of silence, he muttered, "Jeez. We will have to get the hell out of here soon anyway."

"We didn't find it though."

"Yeah, and that makes me even more antsy to get out of here. What if it's a trap?" Stu asked.

Tristan waited until they stepped out of his room, before he slowly stood, walked over to the doorway—where he could stare into the other room—then watched. As the two men headed to the private offices in the back, Tristan silently stepped up behind the one in the rear and held his gun to this intruder's head. "I wouldn't take that next step if I were you," Tristan whispered.

As the man raised his hands slowly, Tristan hit him hard enough on the back of the head to drop him, catching him to muffle the noise, then quickly moving his limp body out of the way. He stepped forward, prepared to face the other man, who still hadn't realized that not finding the USB wasn't his only problem.

"Where the hell can it be?" the man roared.

Tristan smiled and cocked his gun.

Recognizing the sound, the man froze and slowly turned to him. "Shit, where the hell did you come from?"

"Doesn't matter, but where did you come from, and who's paying you to come in here and toss this place, looking for a stupid key?"

The guy's eyes widened, as he realized that Tristan must have heard something. "Where is my fucking partner?"

"Your partner is out cold," Tristan replied, "and I suggest he stay that way for a little bit longer."

"No way, man. If you hurt him," he snapped, "I will have something to say."

"Yeah, you might, especially when—What is he, family or something? Someone you dragged into some trouble?"

The guy paled. "He's my brother-in-law. My sister will kill me."

"Yeah, she sure will. Especially when she finds out you took her husband on a midnight jaunt to make some money, when there isn't any."

"There's money," he declared, his eyes wide. "What are

you talking about? There's always money."

"Everybody involved in this case so far has taken a bullet between the eyes instead of getting paid. Is that what you want?"

Nothing but silence came for a long moment. "I want to get out of this alive."

"You should have thought of that before you came in here then," Jasper interjected, as he came through the rear door at the intruder's back. "So are you Lem or Stu?"

"Lem." He turned to face Jasper. "Now that you're here, don't mind us if we just mosey on out."

Jasper looked over at Tristan. Tristan smiled and shared, "They've got this idea that they can come and go as they want, with no penalty for breaking and entering into a military facility."

"Not like this is any a special place," Lem replied.

"Oh, but it is," Jasper remarked, with a smile, "which begs the question as to how you got onto the compound."

"Oh, Stu and me got a ticket for that," Lem explained. "We do service work on base all the time."

"*Great*, and does your boss know about your B&E sideline?"

"N-n-no," Lem stuttered, "he doesn't know, and I would appreciate it if you didn't tell him."

Tristan snorted at that. "No way you're just walking out of here, so you might as well accept the consequences."

"What do you mean?" Lem glared at him. "It's not as if you guys will stop us."

Tristan looked over at Stu, who was trying to sit up now. "Seriously?" Tristan asked, pointing at his incapacitated friend.

Lem shook his head. "It would be nice if you didn't."

"It would have been nice if you and Stu hadn't come in here and tossed the place either," Jasper stated, then turned and motioned to the MPs behind him. "Lock up these two," he ordered.

Immediately Lem bolted for the door, but two more MPs were stationed there, who quickly snagged him. "We didn't do anything," he roared.

"You and Stu both entered restricted base offices," Tristan explained. "You already admitted that you work for a company and used their privileges and credentials to come in here and do this, looking for a data key you couldn't find, so theft was your intent."

"Then on top of all that," Jasper added, "you told two navy investigators that we can't do anything about it."

"And you're wrong about that, Lem," Tristan confirmed. "You may want to call your families right now before you leave here, so they'll know what happened to you."

Lem frowned at him. "Surely it can't be that bad. They just wanted a USB key, for Christ's sake." He stared at his partner in crime. "You're such a dumb fuck."

Stu glared at his buddy. "If I'm in trouble, it's your fault. You're the one who got me into this," he snarled. "So, when your sister gets on her high horse and bitches me out, I'll just tell her to come talk to you."

"Yeah, you do that," Lem grumbled. "It's not as if she'll talk to you in jail as it is."

"I won't do no jail, so ain't nobody starting that shit with me," Stu muttered. "I didn't do anything."

"Yet you did," Tristan corrected, staring at him. "The military authorities might go a little bit easier on you if you talk."

Immediately silence filled the room, and Lem and Stu

eyed each other for a moment, then looked back at him.

"How about you let us go free and clear, and then we'll talk?" Lem suggested.

"No way because, once you step out of this building, you will take a bullet between the eyes, courtesy of the people who hired you," Tristan pointed out cheerfully, "and we won't get any answers that way."

"You said that before," Lem pointed out in a testy voice, "and I'm telling you that they're not like that."

Jasper shook his head. "Everybody else is in the morgue."

Tristan cut in and confirmed, "I've already told them that, and they don't believe it, though the one might have been sleeping when I had that discussion with his partner-in-crime. Anyway they don't want to believe it. They think they're friends with these guys and know them well. They don't understand how the boss man will kill them because they failed to find the USB, just like the others were killed for failing to do their jobs."

Smiling, Jasper added, "That's not Lem's and Stu's problem, is it? As far as they're concerned, they probably think that whoever is in the morgue did something to deserve being killed. Yet they didn't deserve death," Jasper shared. "Just like you two, those other people didn't realize that failing to do their jobs—or failing to get the infamous key—will have boss man issuing a kill order on you."

"So, just let us have the key," Lem alternatively suggested, "and nobody gets hurt."

"Not happening," Tristan replied, with a smile. "Nice try though."

Stu, the smaller of the two men, got desperate and said, "Look, if we say anything, ... we're dead."

"Exactly," Tristan agreed. "Yet, if you *don't* say anything, you're also dead."

Lem laughed. "Look. I've been dealing with these guys for months. No way they're like that. This was just a simple job. The one even told me that, if we couldn't get the key, … no big deal."

"Oh, did they now?" Jasper snorted. "That's an interesting thing for them to mention. Did they say what they wanted the USB for?"

Lem replied, "Just that they didn't want something of a personal nature released. … Man, I get that too. Shit, I've done some stupid things in my time, and I wished I could have gone back and gotten rid of all the video feeds."

"I bet," Tristan agreed, with a snarky voice. "So, that's what he told you this was, *huh*?"

"Yeah," said Lem. "Some pictures caught him in a bad light, just when he's about to marry somebody. So he didn't want that to screw things up—you know, some big hoity-toity family and all that." He laughed. "She's a looker too. Damn, she's a looker."

"You've met this fiancée?" Tristan asked him.

"*Nah*, but you know, … big high-society wedding coming up, not too many of those in the news right now." Lem fell silent, and Stu just stared at him in horror.

Tristan smiled and asked Stu, "Do you want to confirm that?"

He shook his head. "Man, I don't want anything to do with that conversation. This isn't good."

"Why is that?"

"It's bad," Stu stated. "You shouldn't know anything."

"Maybe we don't know anything truthful and honest. Maybe your partner Lem here is just full of shit."

"I am not," Lem declared. "I might not be the smartest cup in the cupboard, but that guy did something pretty stupid, and he doesn't want to lose his wife-to-be over it. Yet we couldn't find the key." Lem sighed.

Tristan nodded. "You failed to find the key, so what will you do about it now?"

"Keep looking for it wherever he tells us to," Lem muttered. "It's different, looks like a bloody car."

"That's interesting. How would he know what the key even looks like?" Tristan asked.

"Something about … he saw it."

"Maybe he's the one doing the blackmailing?" Tristan asked.

"No," Lem said. "He's the one being blackmailed, and he just didn't dare let it get any further because of the wedding. His father-in-law isn't the kind to stand around and to let that shit happen to the family name."

"Yeah, and what about Trinity? How did she feel?" Tristan took a stab in the dark at the name, as he remembered a big society wedding coming up and a lot of buzz about it, with a military husband-to-be.

"I don't think she thinks very much of it. So, you know her name?" Lem asked.

"Yeah, glad you caught on to that."

"I don't think she knows her fiancé is catting around, and she probably won't bother Daddy about it at all, just as long as she gets her spending money."

"*Right.*" Tristan nodded. "I've met a few of those in my time."

"*Right.*" Stu rolled his eyes, adding his two cents. "I would like to bang a chick like that, but I sure as hell wouldn't want to try and keep one happy paycheck-wise. …

if you know what I mean."

"Man, you can't even keep my own sister happy," Lem complained, staring at his brother-in-law in disgust, "and you might have just got yourself killed."

"Yeah, not likely," Stu countered in a harsh tone.

Stu said, "This is not my fight, not my problem. You're the one who got me into this shit." He snarled and huffed at this partner. "If anybody pays, it'll be you, Lem." Stu just shook his head.

Stu turned to Tristan. "So, now what?" he asked in disgust.

"You tell me. You're the one who's not talking."

Lem chuckled at that. "Yeah, I talked, so I walk out of here free and clear," Lem declared, with a big grin. "Wait until my sister hears that I made a deal and that you're the one stuck holding the bag."

Stu just glared at him, then turned to Tristan and stated, "You know that this is bad news for us, right?"

"I'm telling you how it's bad news no matter which way you look at it," Tristan repeated, "but you knew that going in. You knew exactly that you were up to no good and what the penalty would be. I suspect you were hoping that Lem would get blamed and that you would get out free and clear."

A smile played at Stu's lips. "Not a bad plan."

"Except Lem's the one already talking."

"He always talks. That's the thing," Stu complained. "However, you can't trust anything that comes out of his mouth. He's loose that way."

"I am not." Lem glared at Stu. "You're the one always talking,"

Tristan asked Stu, "The question right now is, do you

confirm what Lem just told us?"

Stu shrugged. "I guess. It's not as if I can deny it now."

"See?" Lem, the big guy, pointed at Stu. "You always talk."

"Yeah, but what you just did was put us in deep trouble." Stu snarled. "If the boss finds out you talked, we're shit out of luck."

Jasper shook his head. "You still don't want to believe it, but you're *both* pretty much doomed either way."

"And if we are"—Stu turned to face Tristan—"then you guys have to look after us."

"Why is that?" Tristan asked, eyeing him with a bored expression. "You're the ones who broke in here. Nobody gives a shit about a couple of two-bit hoods."

"That's not true," Lem spoke up, rejoining the conversation. "We have information."

"What information? You already gave it to us."

Lem opened his mouth and then slammed it shut, knowing that to be true.

Stu turned to his brother in-law and muttered, "You dumb fuck."

"What?" Lem asked. "I didn't tell him about Tony or about the bar where he spends his time or nothing like that," he argued. "We should still bargain with that."

Stu just groaned and looked over at Tristan, who had a big grin on his face.

"Interesting people you hang out with, Stu," Tristan noted, with a bright smile.

"Hey," Lem cried out. "I told my sister not to marry him, but she didn't listen, and now look at the shit I've got to deal with."

"So, what else do you have to bargain with, Stu?" Tristan

asked.

Stu went silent, but Lem spoke up. Again. "Hey, I've got something. It should be worth something," the big man began, looking at Tristan. "Where Tony stays, all kinds of things about him."

"Yeah, so do you know why he wants the key?"

"I told you that already," Lem replied in confusion.

"Have you ever heard the name Mason?" Tristan asked.

"Yeah, that's some guy Tony hates."

Jasper turned to face Lem, staring intently. That caught his interest and Tristan's too. "Any idea why?" Jasper asked.

Lem shook his head. "No, I don't know why, but whatever is between them is bad, as in ugly bad."

"Maybe, but that doesn't tell me anything about what or why."

"I can't tell you that because I don't know," Lem admitted. "I really don't. … All I know is, Tony clams up and gets an ugly look on his face when somebody mentions Mason's name. Just don't know what it's all about though." Lem shrugged. "And, if you're smart, you would stay away from that topic too."

"Wouldn't that be nice? But it's not an option in our case."

"It sucks to be you then," Lem replied. "I just know that Tony has some serious hate for Mason."

"Enough to hire a sniper to take him out?"

Lem considered it. "Maybe, but I don't know anything about that." He shook his head and went on. "If that's what you're after, we don't have any information on that. We just know about the key."

"And you're pretty sure it was Tony's stuff on the key that he wanted to protect?"

Lem shrugged. "I didn't question it, just assumed what he told me was the truth, but who the hell knows with people these days."

"What do you mean?" Tristan asked.

"Everybody lies."

"They sure do," Tristan confirmed, with a wry look at Lem, "including you."

"Hey, I'm just saving my ass to get cleared here," he declared. "We aren't armed or anything. So we didn't come here looking for any trouble."

"No, but you sure found it, didn't you?"

CHAPTER 11

AMARYLIS SLEPT LIKE a log. When she woke the next morning to find herself curled up in her own bed, warm and carefree, she smiled happily and stretched, enjoying just knowing that everything was okay in her world for once. It seemed the stress had been never ending over the last few days, the chaos coming at her nonstop from all directions. She was happy that, for the moment, she could just chill and take a breath.

She checked her phone for messages, and, sure enough, one was from Tristan. It was short and sweet.

Heading to bed, a bit late. Tons of new intel. I'll call you in the morning.

She looked at the time his message had been sent—two in the morning, just as she had suspected his night to go. She swore at that because he would never get any restorative sleep at this rate. She got up slowly, noting she was a little on the sore side—standing too long over her tables—and headed to make coffee. She wasn't even sure who all she was making coffee for because she didn't know whether her guard was outside her door or not.

As she stepped into her kitchen, she looked to see if anybody was around, which didn't make sense as Scott was outside. She made coffee and had a quick shower. After she got dressed, she poured herself a cup and sat down to relax but couldn't. She still had heard nothing from Tristan or the guard. So she got up, checked her peephole but saw nothing. Then she looked through her front window.

No sign of Scott or anybody. Maybe he'd been called away, or maybe he was sitting in his car or walking around the perimeter of the building at the back right now. That would make sense.

She sent a message to Tristan, sharing that she was up, and she hoped he got some sleep. With that, she quickly rummaged in her kitchen and found enough bread to put on some toast, but that's about all she had for food. Just as she was buttering the toast, her phone rang. "Hey," she answered cheerfully. "How are you feeling?"

"I'm doing pretty well," he murmured. "Got a bit of a headache, but that's life."

"You're right. Life is that way sometimes," she agreed. "Everything go okay last night?"

"It did. How about you?"

"I caught some sleep, which for me is starting to feel like something I never, ever get, but the wine last night at dinner helped, I think," she shared. "So I'm doing just fine."

"Oh, good. Sleep helps, doesn't it?" he said, with a laugh.

"I haven't seen Scott yet this morning, but I presume he's outside somewhere."

"I'll check in with him. Do you normally talk to him?"

"Yeah, some. After spending a day with him at work, we interacted a bit, even if he wasn't in the morgue itself. Plus, he drove me home last night, so we have been talking. Normally when I'm at home, he's outside my door, but not this morning," she said, yawning, "I'm just checking to confirm everything is still okay."

"I'll find out for you." And Tristan quickly hung up.

She didn't think anything of it, just sat here enjoying her coffee, until Tristan called her back.

"When did you last see Scott?"

"When he brought be home after we left the restaurant. Why?"

"Nobody's heard from him this morning," Tristan shared. "You need to lock yourself inside your apartment and stay put."

"Oh, no. No, no, no," she wailed. "Hurting Scott is not allowed. He's just a nice young kid."

"I get that, but we need to find him first. Don't panic. For all we know, he's sound asleep somewhere. We couldn't get him relief on time last night, so he had to work a double shift. However, someone should have shown up later, and I'm not sure they did. I'm still tracking people down, so please don't panic yet. I just don't want to track you down too, if you leave the apartment."

"Right," she muttered, as she sat back and looked down at her toast that no longer had the same appeal.

She didn't want anything to happen to that young man. Scott was a good kid, but he was still just a kid. She waited tensely for another twenty minutes, and, when no return phone call came, she bolted to her feet and started pacing inside her apartment.

She didn't know where Scott could have gone or what trouble he could have gotten into, but, with all the chaos going on here at the base, it didn't take much imagination to think that something bad may have happened to him.

She paced for several moments, and, when Tristan finally called her back, he said, "So, I just got off the phone, and Scott is in the hospital."

"Oh my God," she cried out. "What happened?"

"He's alive, but he took a blow to the head."

"When? Where?"

"We think it happened sometime last night. The security detail that was supposed to relieve him got their wires crossed somehow, and nobody showed up. So we don't know what time Scott was attacked. As it is, someone was sent to check on him when they realized this morning that nobody had relieved him overnight. They couldn't contact him via phone, so they searched around for him earlier this morning, and that's when they found him."

She sat there, tears running down her face. She thought she might have been able to hide it, but Tristan heard her sobs.

"He's alive, Amarylis," he reminded her.

"Yes," she murmured, "and, for that, I'm damn grateful, but what the hell?"

"I know. I will head to the hospital first, and then I'll come to your place."

"No, pick me up. I want to go to the hospital with you." He hesitated and she added, "Either that, or I'm going there myself."

"Of course you are," he muttered, a note of humor in his tone.

"Just as you would," she pointed out.

"I'll be there in five," he said, "but remember. Don't open that damn door to anybody."

She didn't say anything but waited at the door, fully dressed, ready for Tristan to show up. When he didn't show up on time, she texted him several times.

Finally he called her back. "Look. I'm stuck out here near the parking lot. The traffic's been a bitch. I promise nothing's wrong. I'm just running late."

She sagged back in place and waited for him to get to her door.

When a knock finally came, Tristan called out, "It's me. Let me in." She hurriedly opened it. As he walked in, he saw the tears in her eyes. He just opened his arms, and she raced into them.

"Oh my God," she whispered, when she could finally talk. "This is just too harsh."

"I know, and it's definitely something we're still sorting out."

"Why would somebody even do that?"

"Obviously they didn't want him here, and that would mean that they were doing something that they wanted hidden, but I just don't know what," he admitted. "With any luck, the scout coming to find Scott ran off whatever bad guys were here. Come on. Let's lock up and head over to the hospital, so you can see him."

And that's what they did. When they got to his room, Scott was awake and pissed. He took one look at Amarylis and asked, "Jeez, are you okay?"

She nodded. "I'm fine, but what happened to you?"

He frowned. "After I dropped you off, maybe a couple hours later, I went out into the trees to take a leak," he explained, "and I didn't even see it coming. I heard this weird *whoosh* and lights out." He gingerly put his hand to the back of his head. "When I woke up, I was terrified they'd gotten to you."

"They didn't." Then she winced. "At least not yet."

"And they won't," Tristan vowed, standing at her side.

"Jeez, you've got to look after her," Scott said. "I don't know what the hell these guys want, but they're adamant."

"A little more than adamant, considering we had a break-in at our investigation offices last night too."

"They must want whatever it is they're looking for pretty badly."

"Oh, they want it pretty badly all right," Tristan agreed, with a nod, "but they aren't getting it."

"Good," Scott snapped. "And, after this knock on the head, now I for sure don't want those assholes getting it."

Tristan smiled. "What you need to do now is get better and get yourself out of here."

"I would love to," Scott muttered, "but the doc won't let me go."

"Of course not," Amarylis noted. "Head injuries can be very tricky." Scott scowled at her, and she shrugged. "Don't glare at me. You have to talk to your doctor about setting you free, but, if you were my patient, I wouldn't let you go either."

Scott pointed a finger at her. "That's because you see me as a kid, and you don't want me to get hurt."

She glared at him. "I don't want you to get *more* hurt," she retorted.

He smiled. "Hey, this one was pretty easy. I took a knock, but it's not as if he was gonna kill me." At that, he turned and looked at Tristan. "Wait. How come he didn't kill me?"

"I don't know, Scott. I just don't know—maybe because you're young." Tristan shook his head. "However, we'll take it as a good thing regardless."

"Yeah, well, that's a pisser in itself, isn't it?"

Amarylis frowned at him. "What? Now you wanted to

get killed?"

"No, … I obviously don't want to get killed," he scoffed. "Yet, if they didn't do what they would normally do just because they see me as kid, … it's insulting."

She shook her head, then looked over at Tristan, who was grinning wildly. "Christ, you're all nuts," she muttered.

"Yeah, we probably are," Scott admitted cheerfully.

"Now you've got your first war wound," she snapped, glaring at him, "but you shouldn't be quite so happy about it."

"Hey, you're not hurt, so it's all good."

She smiled at that. "I do thank you for taking such good care of me."

He glared. "I'm just surprised he didn't come up after you."

"Me too," she replied.

"So, what is our theory on that?" Scott asked, looking at Tristan.

"Maybe our guy scouting around for you disturbed the bad guy's plans or maybe they thought she would be under guard inside her apartment as well," Tristan suggested.

"Yeah, either makes sense. So then what? They just sit back and see what happens next at her apartment or at her office—or yours?"

"Maybe," Tristan replied, with a nod. "That could very well be it."

She glared at the two of them. "They sure as hell better not come after me again," she snapped. "I'm pretty fed up with this whole thing."

"Yeah, we all are too," Scott noted, with a smile. "So, we need this to come to an end, one that finishes it, not just an end that leaves us with no answers."

Tristan nodded. "We have the two guys who broke into our offices last night," Tristan shared, with a smile, "We got some information from them, and we're hoping to get more."

"Good." Scott snarled. "Any assholes come back after me, I'm taking them down."

They left him still in his feisty mood, which in some ways relieved Amarylis. As they walked outside, she asked, "Is that all talk coming from Scott?"

"Not all of it," Tristan replied. "Some of it is just relief, and, whatever happened, he did survive. Now he's got something he can brag about," he added, with a chuckle.

She shook her head, "That head wound is nothing to laugh about."

"No, it isn't, which is why he's damn happy to be where he is. Nobody's releasing him anytime soon," Tristan said, "so don't you worry about that."

She smiled. "He's a good kid, and I hate to see him get hurt."

"He's already been hurt, and he's damn lucky it wasn't a lot worse. So, with any luck, he won't come up against something like that again."

She nodded and smiled, as they headed out of the hospital. "Now what?"

"You're not going to work." She stopped in her tracks and frowned at him. He nodded. "Dr. Cox has already been briefed on all that's happened, and he's the one who doesn't want you bringing that shit to work."

She groaned. "Oh, *great*, so now *I'm* bringing this crap to work, am I? How come it's all on me now?"

"It's not that you're responsible, but we must consider other people who could get caught up as collateral damage," he pointed out. "Your coworkers at the morgue."

She sighed. "So where am I going then?"

"You're coming with me to my office."

"Oh, *great*," she muttered. "What is this, *take your kid to work* day?"

He stated, "I don't know what *kid* you think you might resemble, but you're all woman to me." She flushed bright red at that, and he chuckled. "Come on. This isn't how you wanted your day to go, but—"

"Definitely not how I want my day to go," she grumbled.

"But you'll behave because you know people are out there, ready to take a hit to protect you. Therefore, you've got to do your part to make sure it's not in vain."

She glared at him. "That, sir, was a low blow."

He gave her an infectious smile. "Hey, whatever works. Right about now everybody in my world would just as soon see you locked down and going nowhere, until this is all sorted out. So don't expect too many people to give you any leniency to be out and about."

"It's not about leniency," she clarified. "I just don't want to be a prisoner."

LOOKING AT HER, his gaze darkened, as he took a moment to consider whether he should voice what he was thinking. And, since it was important, he did.

"I don't want you dead."

Opposing his stance on her death was a hard position to argue, and, as Tristan had hoped, Amarylis wasn't putting up much of an argument against him. Generally she was incredibly cooperative, but it was evident that seeing her young guard in the hospital had hit her hard. "Scott will be fine, you know?"

She just nodded and didn't say anything more. When they got to his office, she still hadn't talked very much. He looked over at her. "Look. If you don't want to be here, I can probably arrange for a guard someplace for you, though probably not at your apartment right now."

"No, that's fine," she muttered, shaking her head. "I just need to remind myself that this isn't my deal and that I'm caught up in something I don't have the skill set to take on. Thus, I need to be grateful that you are here to keep me safe."

Surprised but happy at her change of heart, he nodded. "Good. Please don't sneak away or do anything stupid or heroic that will cause any of us to panic and to expend resources figuring out where you are."

"I wasn't planning on it," she said, looking over at him.

"I get that, but not everybody always thinks clearly at times like this, and what we don't want is to inadvertently create more confusion or chaos."

She nodded and still didn't say anything.

Hoping that she was good to go, he took her into the office, where she passed by Sam and Morgan. She smiled at the men and greeted them. "Hey." They smiled back. As soon as Amarylis and Tristan reached the office he used, Tristan got a phone call and a request to go back out front.

He groaned. "Now I'm about to get grilled by the men."

"Why?" she asked.

"I suspect it's mostly because they don't want you here."

"Oh, *great*," she muttered, staring at him. "That's not guaranteed to make me feel very good."

He smiled. "Not because you're a danger to them, but because they don't want you here, where you could be in further trouble. We had a break-in right here last night, remember?"

She nodded slowly. "I still don't understand how the intruders thought they would get the key."

"I suspect they were sent in as a test of sorts, to see how they handled themselves. And, if they found the key, all the better."

"But, if the intruders could identify the man who wanted the USB, why the hell would that man risk using those two guys?"

"I'm not so sure that the guy they think they know is the one who's involved." She shook her head at that, and he laughed. "Apparently the deal with our two burglars was arranged through an intermediary, and they just assumed it was him on the USB. Thus, they assumed that he was the one they were helping, thinking he was some bigwig figure who would bring them some money down the road."

"Who are these guys? That sounds like sheer stupidity."

He smiled. "I don't know about sheer stupidity, but let's just say it's not the smartest move somebody would make."

"Yeah, no kidding," she replied. "So many things can go wrong with that picture."

He smiled. "Not only go wrong but, in theory, they don't have a clue about an awful lot, and I think that's what's happening here."

"So these two bumpkins were just the hired help? Like those terrorist groups, with each part of the op segregated, knowing only their task to do? If so, whether stupid or part of a bigger op, how much of their story is worth listening to?"

"Exactly." He chuckled cheerfully. "We're sifting through it, trying to confirm what we've got so far. Meanwhile, settle in here for a while."

"So, if I had my laptop," she noted, "I could get some work done here."

"I can have it brought to you, if you want."

She looked over at him and nodded. "If you're okay with that, it would be a good compromise."

"I'll get it. Is it at home?"

"No, it's at the office. I can get Dr. Cox to have it ready for me." She quickly called him and explained what she wanted.

He agreed. "I'll get it ready for you. Just send one of the men over to pick it up."

And with that done, she smiled at Tristan and sat back. "All I need now is an office."

"You can have an office," he said, as he got up. "Do you want mine?"

"I want one that is private and won't get broken into."

He burst out laughing. "I think we all want one of those."

She nodded. "I imagine you do, but, all joking aside, anyplace will work."

"Good enough." He smiled. "Give me a few minutes." Then he stepped out of the office and left her alone.

He walked out to the main office, where Sam and Morgan sat at their desks. "Amarylis needs an office to work in. Any concerns about one room versus another?"

They turned, their eyebrows raised. Sam spoke up, an attitude evident in his tone. "How long is she here for?"

"I don't know. Have you got a better suggestion? The guard outside her apartment was attacked last night, so I hardly think her sitting at home is the best location for her."

"Yeah, but that's only because you've got plans for her."

Tristan frowned at Sam. "Your attitude already wants me to stomp the hell out of you, but the idea that you would insult somebody like her in this situation is beyond belief. I suggest you get a hold of whatever it is that's pissing you off and deal with it, and you better do it fast." Tristan then turned to Morgan. "Do you give a shit about what office she uses? Otherwise I'll just park her in the one beside mine."

"Why don't you just put her in yours?" Sam asked, with a sneer.

Fed up, he turned to reply, but Morgan intervened. "Let it go, both of you. This isn't the time or the place."

"Maybe not," Sam conceded, "but obviously he's another one who thinks he's running the show, and I'm getting damn tired of it."

Tristan shook his head as Jasper walked in the front door.

"What's the problem now?" Jasper asked.

"Just looking for a place to put Amarylis, so she can work."

"Right, we can't have her going into her office, can we?"

"No, Dr. Cox asked her not to be there in order to keep the rest of the staff safer."

"Why didn't you say so?" Sam retorted, yet with a smile this time. "Damn, you don't have to act like you're some kamikaze all the time, always working alone."

"Yet it feels that way," Tristan declared, turning on him. "Every time I'm here, I have to break through your walls to get anything done."

Sam glared at him, and, without another word, he turned and walked out of the building.

Morgan sighed. "I get that he's a pain in the ass some-times, but he is a good investigator."

Neither Tristan nor Jasper said anything to that. Tristan turned to Jasper. "Can we finally start getting some work done, please?"

And with a slight head movement from Jasper, they headed over to the in-house jail to visit Terry, the intruder they'd captured at Amarylis's apartment. Finding him still uncooperative, Jasper and Tristan next visited Lem and Stu, the two guys who had broken into their investigative offices. When they walked in, Stu hopped up.

"Look. I need to get out of here," Stu explained. "You don't understand. My wife will be pissed."

Jasper shook his head. Lem groaned. "See? He's not the most brilliant guy."

Stu pointed a finger at his brother-in-law. "You know perfectly well she'll be pissed."

Lem winced and nodded. "Yeah, she will, and these guys already know everything they need to know, so they don't need to be here asking us more questions."

Tristan turned to Jasper, as they both moved farther from these cells. "They didn't get any smarter overnight," Jasper muttered, "but that's no surprise. I was hoping Terry would talk."

"He started talking but has stopped, … unless maybe he finds out," Tristan whispered, "that Lem and Stu are our guests as well and are talking."

Jasper grinned. "That wouldn't be the worst idea in the world."

"Right," Tristan agreed, "all we have to do is just let them see each other."

"Yet these two might not even know who he is."

"Maybe not," Tristan conceded, "but what are the chances that they know Terry as Tony? It's worth a shot for sure."

"Let me go put Terry in a different cell," Jasper shared, with a smile, "and I'll be back in a few minutes. You go chat with Stu and Lem." Jasper winked and was off.

With that, Tristan returned to stand in front of Lem and Stu's cells.

Lem asked, "So what are you two talking about? Ready to release us?"

"We're checking how much truth we can verify in your story. We're sure as hell won't believe anything blindly."

"We already told you who's involved," Lem wailed, with an exasperated tone.

"And yet, as far I can tell, you guys didn't tell us the truth. You told us that Tony was the manager at the pool hall."

Lem nodded. "Yeah, that's right."

Yet Stu's gaze narrowed, and Tristan could see him thinking. Stu finally asked, "You think Tony wasn't the manager?"

"Oh, I'm thinking he managed you quite nicely," Tristan quipped, "but that doesn't mean that anything Tony had to say was the truth. Tony just let you think that you were working for him and not some other guy."

Lem and Stu shared a glance, then frowned at Tristan. Stu shared, "That wouldn't be good."

"No, it wouldn't be good at all. It would also mean that you were working for somebody you don't know, and for somebody maybe you shouldn't trust."

Lem narrowed his gaze. "But you don't know that for sure."

"How can I, when we don't have all the information on your *manager* friend," Tristan pointed out, enunciating the word clearly.

Stu flushed. "We told you everything."

"No, you didn't. You told me what you wanted me to know." Tristan grinned. "You haven't exactly been forthcoming beyond that."

"We can't give you everything," Stu protested. "We would have nothing left to bargain with."

"You have nothing to bargain with now," Tristan snapped.

Lem stared at him. "You think we got roped?"

"I don't know if you got roped as much as you eagerly signed up for something you shouldn't have," he pointed out, looking over at him. "I don't know which is the case because, when we talk to people, we get one version, and then you turn around and talk among yourselves and give us a completely different version."

Stu shrugged, sticking with his tight-lipped position. "We've got to keep some things secret, don't we?"

"I wouldn't at this point in time," Tristan said. "This guy who hired you isn't necessarily the guy who you thought hired you."

"I get what you're saying. I just don't see what the point would be."

"The point would be that, if you don't know who did the hiring, you might be one step removed, or he is."

"Sure, but it's not as if we haven't been around these guys."

"And that's why you assumed that he was making the arrangements, right?"

"Yes," Lem replied, carefully looking at him. "I still

don't know that he wasn't. We only have your word for it."

Tristan nodded. "I highly doubt that Tony was the big boss. He just involved himself in the hiring process for you guys."

"No, of course not, that's what the boss has Tony for."

"Right, and what if this guy was hiring you for somebody else, and you just didn't know it? Maybe what he does is hire people, but he didn't hire you for the job you were thinking it was."

"It was to get that USB key," Lem argued, standing up, waving his arms about, and clearly getting frustrated now. "We just wanted to get paid."

"Exactly, so you're happy to do what you needed to do to get money, and he was happy because he got two clowns to come in here on a military base, with the ability to get in because of your day jobs, just hoping you might find something he's looking for. Or maybe not what *he's* looking for but that somebody else is looking for."

"Sure, but again it don't matter who the USB is for."

"It's a slight difference from your point of view," Tristan acknowledged. "All I'm saying is that the actual end boss may not be who you think it is."

Lem frowned. "Okay." Lem sat down now, staring at Tristan. "I see what you're saying. It's important that *you* get the right guy, I suppose."

"We have five bodies that we know of, plus the kidnapping and torture of a military investigator, plus a sniper shooting another military official," Tristan explained. "So it's important to find the big boss man behind it all."

Lem paled at that news. "We had nothing to do with all that," he stated.

"You got any idea who was involved in the sniper shooting?"

Lem winced and nodded. "Yeah, but I haven't seen that guy in a while now."

"I don't suppose his name was Drew, was it?"

Lem just stared for a moment. "Why do you ask us if you already know?"

"Because Drew is dead. His body was found a few days ago. He had been shot, or maybe he shot himself. That investigation is pending, but, either way, he's still dead."

"No, no, no. … We knew he went missing, but we didn't have nothing to do with no murders," Lem stammered, nervously backing away from Tristan, but physically unable to put any more distance between them because he was already against the back wall of his cell. "Jeez." He turned and looked at Stu, his brother-in-law, who was staring at Lem in shock.

Stu asked, "What did you get me into?"

Lem roared, "Nothing, nothing like this, I swear. No way, I wouldn't put my own life or my sister's life in jeopardy."

That slowed down Stu slightly, as he pondered that. They both turned to look at Tristan. "Why the hell would you even think we were involved with murders and snipers and torture?"

"Somebody is sure as hell involved," Tristan noted, "and we're not *thinking* anything. We already have the proof. We're just finding out who is ultimately behind it all. We have the sniper shooting of a high-ranking navy official and the kidnapping and torture of a navy investigator to solve, in addition to all these other murders and related crimes."

"And you think all of that has something to do with that USB key?" Lem asked Tristan.

Tristan looked over at him and asked, "What do you think?"

Lem sat down suddenly. "Oh my God. ... I don't feel so good."

"I wonder why?" Tristan asked. "When you screw up, you really screw up, don't you?"

Lem shook his head. "Don't even say it that way," he muttered, hanging his head. "I didn't have nothing to do with this."

"Yet you did, and you got Stu involved as well."

Lem looked over at his brother-in-law and again shook his head. "We were told it was no big deal. We were told that we wouldn't get caught, as long as we got out before the allotted time was up. We were told it was a simple B&E. Just pick up a USB key shaped like a car and go."

"Yet you were supposed to be in and out in twenty minutes, right?"

"Yeah, something like that." Then he stopped and stared, his eyes wide open, "How did you know?"

"I heard you two talking, when you first came in."

He stared at him and moaned. "Jeez. We were caught inside immediately. So we would've never got out of here cleanly, would we?"

"Nope, you wouldn't," Tristan replied. "I was giving you enough time to hang yourselves." Lem just glared at him, as Tristan shrugged. "What did you expect me to do? Let you walk, when you were obviously involved in this mess on base. Meanwhile, the body count and injuries just keep going up."

Lem shook his head. "Christ, I don't know how it all got so bad." Just then his eyes widened, as somebody caught his attention. Lem jumped forward and frantically yelled,

"That's him. That's him."

Tristan turned to see Terry, the intruder they had captured inside Amarylis's apartment. "Him who?" he asked Lem, looking to get clarification on the record.

"That's the guy who hired us. That's the manager, Tony." Lem looked over at Jasper, who was leading the man to a cell farther down the hallway.

Jasper stopped the MPs guarding Tony, aka Terry, and declared, "Look at that. These two just ID'd you as somebody who hired them to do a B&E into our offices right here on base."

Tony looked at the two men behind bars and sneered. "Not likely. Who would ever hire those bozos? They couldn't even do a simple job."

At that, Lem replied, "You didn't even know who you were doing the job for, and you sure as hell didn't let us know who we were really working for, did you?"

"You didn't need to know," Tony stated, with a shrug. "And look. You're in jail. You got caught. You did a piss-ass shitty job of it."

"Yeah, well, we might not have been quite so bad if we'd understood our roles."

"Are you kidding? You might have been even worse," Tony snapped, with a sneer. "Look at the two of you, … completely useless."

"That's hardly fair," Lem argued, glaring at Tony. "You told us the key *was* there, not that it might be."

"I was told it was there," he corrected. "Obviously you didn't find it." Then he stopped and asked them, "Or did you?"

Lem shook his head. "No, we didn't find it."

"And that's because," Tristan shared cheerfully, "it's not

in our offices, which we've been very clear about all along."

Tony ignored him.

It was fascinating to watch these men close up like this. They were almost friends but not quite, more like acquaintances. They were men caught up in circumstances beyond their understanding and yet had been hired to do a job, be it together, apart, or something else.

Then Tristan suddenly understood and studied the man they knew as Terry, but Lem knew as Tony. "So, you were hired to find that key, and you've been busy hiring other people to hit the places you couldn't get to." Tony didn't respond. "You hired these guys because you were getting pretty desperate. Yet they had easy access to the base, and that made sense to you."

"It should have made sense to them too," Tony replied bitterly. "But then you realize that there's just no making sense for some people."

The two men stiffened and glared at him.

Tony shrugged. "Look at you guys. It should have been simple."

"If it was that simple, why didn't you do it?" Lem snapped.

"Oh, right." Tony sneered. "I was a little busy dealing with other aspects of the same issue."

Lem muttered, "If you had told us that more shit was involved, we might have been able to do something about it."

Tony gave a bitter laugh. "No way. Guys like you? They never get it. It's all we can do to get you to understand the basics," he sneered, "and now look at you, both sitting in jail."

"Look at you," Lem retorted. "You're in the same jail, so

it's not as if you're in any better position. At least we have some information we can trade off."

Tony snarled at them, then turned and looked at Tristan. "What do you care? If you weren't sleeping with that chick, it wouldn't make a difference."

"For the record, I'm not sleeping with *that chick*," he shared, staring him down, as his gaze narrowed. "Interesting that you think that I am. Regardless, I protect the innocent."

"Hell, I can see the signs."

"*Wanting* to sleep with a chick and *sleeping* with that chick are two different things," Tristan pointed out.

Tony laughed. "Doesn't matter," he said, shaking his head. "You think you've got all the people I hired, but you're wrong, and you'll find out soon enough."

"Oh, that's nice to know," Tristan noted, refusing to turn and look behind him to the office where Amarylis was working. "How many did you hire?"

"As many as I figured I needed and more," Tony stated. "One of them should get the job done." He turned to look at Lem and Stu in the nearby cell, still sitting there, listening in, and snarled again. "It's obvious that these bozos couldn't do the job."

Lem stiffened, but he didn't say anything, as he watched the conversation between Tristan and the man who had hired Lem and Stu.

"You do know that you will get your ass kicked before this is over," Tony vowed.

"Don't know and don't believe it," Tristan stated cheerfully. "You guys threaten people constantly, I suppose, but very few can make good on those promises," he pointed out, with a laugh, "except me."

And, with that, the MPs pushed Terry, aka Tony, into

his new jail cell.

Tristan stopped them and called out, "What would it take for you to own up to being the asshole you are?"

"It would take a lot," Tony declared, with a chuckle. "Why? What do you care?"

"The question is, why do *you* care? Why are you doing this?"

"Money," he replied. "My reason is always the same, money."

"When is it enough? Money, I mean."

"I don't have enough, so I can't tell you that," Tony stated, with a snort. "I'm not some do-gooder like you, who just has to sit here and justify my paycheck."

"Me?" Tristan asked. "What do I have to do with all this?"

"You're the one who's hunting me. You're the one who's stopping me, but you don't even know what the hell is going on or how powerful any of this is."

"No, but it would sure be nice if somebody just told me."

"Nobody will *just tell you*. You have to figure it out for yourself. You haven't got all the answers, and, at this rate, you won't either." Tony laughed. "I may get the last laugh after all. Meanwhile, you better watch that girlfriend of yours." And, with that, he sauntered into his new cell, the two MPs on either side of him.

Tristan felt the anger vibrating through him.

Jasper stepped up and murmured, "Don't let him get to you."

"Too late," Tristan answered, his tone harsh.

"But that's what Tony wants. Instead use that anger to get some answers, to take action in some way."

"Not only is my anger what he wants, it's what he's got, and that means he's still after her." Tristan turned to reassure himself that she was here and safe. He left the cell area and entered the office area. His gaze suddenly widened. "Where the hell is she?" he asked, spinning around, looking for Amarylis.

He raced into the office where he had left her but found no sign of her. He stepped out, looked at the two men across from the office, and asked, "Did you see anything happening here?"

They both frowned at him and asked, "What?"

He turned to Jasper, who had followed him here. "Where did she go? What happened?"

Jasper squeezed his shoulder. "Take it easy now."

"How can I take it easy?" he snapped. Tristan spun around, his fists at the ready, when Jasper gave him a hard shake.

Tristan took a moment, then shook his head. "She was right here," Tristan said, "right here. So where the hell could she be?"

CHAPTER 12

AMARYLIS WOKE UP on the bare floor, a headache pounding through her brain. She groaned at the agony, wondering who the hell was rattling the drums inside her head.

Then a man laughed and said, "You haven't seen nothing yet."

She groaned and shifted in the dim lighting, so she could put a face to the voice. She didn't recognize him, yet she did. She frowned. "I don't even know who you are."

"Good," he replied in a genial voice. "I was hoping you wouldn't recognize me."

She tried hard and stared at him, but recognition just wasn't coming, yet something about his face was familiar. She sagged back and closed her eyes. "Did you have to hit me so hard?"

"I didn't have time to weigh out whether you needed a hard conk or a light conk," he explained, with a chuckle. "I only had so much time to kidnap you right out from underneath someone close by and not have anybody notice."

She opened her eyes and nodded, remembering now. "You walked into the temporary office I was using, supposedly to show me another place to work because a meeting was happening."

"That's right, and you saw a part of the meeting."

"Yes," she agreed, "I saw a bunch of people in the office."

"There were, indeed, so I needed to get you out of there."

"Why?" she asked, looking at him intently and wishing her brain would cooperate. She closed her eyes as the pain kicked in again.

"Got a headache?" he asked.

He couldn't seem to speak of her discomfort without chuckling. "I do, and, seeing how you caused it, I highly doubt you're interested in helping me fix it."

"Ooh, feisty, aren't you?"

Something about that voice reminded her that she'd heard it before.

"Still trying to figure it out? You would be smart if you didn't," he told her. "Then I can keep you alive a little bit longer."

"A little bit longer?" she repeated, frowning at him. "I don't think you intend on keeping me alive at all."

"Intent and planning are two separate things. It would be nice if we can keep you alive, but I don't think that'll work out so well."

"Of course not," she stated, with a nod. "That won't suit your plans, will it?"

"No, it sure won't, and it's good of you to understand."

"It's difficult to understand when you haven't explained anything," she murmured, hoping he would at least share some of it, though she doubted that he would. Guys like this, they were just ego-tripping, but maybe she could use that to her advantage.

"You see," her kidnapper continued, "the one prisoner they brought through the main room, they'd had picked him up the other night. He hired a whole pile of us to get that damn key. If we couldn't get the key, we were supposed to at least get you."

"Why?" she asked, twisting slightly to look at him, "I don't have the key."

"No, but you do know something about where it is."

"No," she countered, "I don't. I knew where it was, waiting to be processed with the rest of the crime scene evidence at the lab, but it was picked up by the investigators."

"So, it is here then," he pounced.

"No, it's not," she stated pointedly. "It was deemed too dangerous to keep here, deemed too much incentive for somebody to go off half-cocked and decide they should have it instead."

He stared at her and nodded. "That would be the smart thing for them to do, but I don't think they're that smart."

"That's just too damn bad," she said. "I don't have any control over what you think or over what they did, but I can tell you the key is not here, and I don't know where it is. Yet, no matter how many times we tell you, nobody wants to listen."

"That's because nobody believes you."

"No, that's because nobody wants to believe us. You all seem to think that just because you want it to be here, it is, therefore, here."

"I don't give a shit regardless," he snapped, "but, now that I've got you, I will get paid anyway."

"And yet you just told me how the guy who hired you is being held by the navy investigators. So how are you getting paid if he's sitting in jail?"

"Because he works for someone else," her captor said, with a smile. "You don't think this is a closed case, and it's quite so simple as that, do you?"

"It would be nice if it was," she noted, "considering that multiple murders have been committed over some stupid USB key. Right?"

"I would think you would want the murders to stop," her captor said. "Why don't you want it to stop? You're one of those nice people who think everything should be sweet and kind and that nobody should ever suffer."

"I don't know where you got that idea," she shared, wincing at her pounding headache, wishing to kill this bastard herself. "Considering the way my head is feeling, you are definitely out to lunch because there is nothing I would like more right now than to cause you a little suffering."

He laughed. "Ha, now you want to make it sound like you're some tough person," he suggested, "but you're not. You're nothing but a pushover."

"*Right, just a pushover.*" She groaned as the pain shifted with her movement again.

"If you didn't keep moving around, it wouldn't hurt so much."

"*Great,*" she quipped. "*Who knew?*"

"You've got some spirit. I like that," he declared, looking at her with interest. "Maybe if you're good, I'll keep you."

"What, as a pet?" she asked, turning to stare at him. "Is that how little respect your mama raised you to have for women?"

"Oh no, you don't get to bring my mama into this," he said, with a hard smile. "Besides, that woman was a damn bitch. She didn't teach me nothing."

"I can see that," she said. "When you start talking about keeping a woman as a pet, obviously your mother didn't teach you anything."

"Nothing worth knowing anyway," he stated. "Besides, you're nothing but trouble, so no way I want you around."

"Great, so let me go."

"No way, I've got to deliver you and get my money."

"Then what?" she asked, curiosity in her voice.

He laughed. "Then I'm out of here. Time for a new job, a new area, a new identity. The whole nine yards."

She frowned, a sudden worry taking over. "Is he paying you that much?" she asked, her voice barely above a whisper.

"He is," he agreed, smiling at her, "because they think you have the goods."

"But I don't. I already told you that," she repeated, trying to figure out where she was. She was in a small windowless room, but she couldn't tell what it was used for. No furniture was here, no boxes, no nothing at all. She was sitting on the floor, apparently waiting for someone to show up. "I gather he's coming here to collect me?" she asked.

"Yeah, he sure is. Promise to be good for him, won't you?"

"*Yeah, sure,*" she said in a mocking tone.

"He won't care if you aren't. He won't. I guess he'll probably just pop you one if you're too much trouble, just like I had to."

"If you keep beating up on me, won't you have a hard time getting your money?"

He turned, giving her a hard expression. "You do anything to jeopardize my money, and I'll make sure you never get out of here, no matter how much he's paying me."

"Right, so in other words, you're all about money and

nothing else."

"That's right, and don't you forget it," he snarled. "Now we have to get moving, so get up." She rose slowly, slightly wobbly on her feet. He grabbed her by the arm and steadied her. "No funny stuff."

"I couldn't even begin to do any funny stuff," she said, as he shoved her forward. "I can barely walk as it is."

"You better suck it up and do a better job of it than you are right now," he snapped. "Don't think I will carry you either. That isn't happening."

He shoved her forward, causing her to stumble. He grabbed her before she fell, holding her steady for a moment while she regained her balance. "I will tell you this once. Keep moving or I'll dump you to the ground myself."

Enough force was behind his words that she believed him, yet he wouldn't get any money by bruising and battering the merchandise. So she was pretty sure that no matter what he threatened, it was all just a boast. She didn't challenge him though. "Look. Unless you want me to puke, you have to give me a chance to adjust to that blow to my head," she shared. "You shouldn't have hit me quite so hard."

"I'll hit you a hell of a lot harder if you don't get moving," he snarled, as he kept pushing her forward. She tried, she did, but she was dizzy, and her head was hurting even more with every step. When she started to flag, he cried out, "What the hell is wrong with you?"

She whispered, "My head ..." And she started to fall again.

"God damn it." He pulled her upright, swung her up into his arms and partially onto his shoulder and proceeded walking down the hallway. As soon as he did, she unhooked an earring and dropped it behind them. As soon as they turned a corner, she dropped the next one. They went through a set of double doors, and she groaned as he dropped her onto her feet again. "Now, see if you can walk."

She took a couple tentative steps.

"Good, that's better."

"It is better, yes," she whispered, "but it sure as hell isn't good yet."

"This is as good as it'll get for you," he snarled. "Christ, I can't believe they even want you."

"Who said they did?" she asked, closing her eyes. "As far as I'm concerned, this is just a fishing expedition, trying to find that damn USB key."

"Maybe it is. Maybe it isn't. That's not my problem," he said. "They told me that you were worth big money, so I'm bringing you in."

"*Great*," she muttered to herself. "I'm worth *big money*. Who knew?"

"You're not kidding. If I would have realized that earlier, I could have picked you up a hell of a long time ago."

She stiffened at that, then turned to look at him.

He caught her gaze and shook his head. "If you figure out who I am, you're in even more trouble."

"*More* trouble? You're already going to kill me."

"No, I'm not, but these guys will."

"*Nice*," she muttered. "Nice people you hang out with."

"Not so much but that's not my problem. Now keep walking."

Nodding, she turned and moved stiffly in the direction he pointed.

"Pick up the pace," he snarled.

She glared at him. "What's the matter? You worried you

might miss your deadline … for selling your kidnap victim?" When his expression turned furious, she realized she was in danger of getting her head smacked again, but putting up no resistance seemed completely wrong as well. So she would certainly not be a compliant victim.

He growled at her. "I don't want anybody catching up with us."

She stopped. "Oh, you mean somebody coming to rescue me? You mean, like Tristan?"

"Yeah, that's exactly what I mean," he stated. "I don't need Tristan interfering."

"I hardly think *interfering* is the correct term," she clarified, with a smile, "particularly when it's my head on the block."

He sneered. "If you weren't sleeping with him, it wouldn't be such a problem. I might not have even done this."

She shook her head and cried out, "Jeez, I'm not sleeping with him." She stared at her captor. "What is this, some misguided jealousy?"

"No, of course not," he replied, with a wave of his hand, "but anything to get back at that asshole suits me."

And, with that hint, it clicked, and now she knew where she'd seen her captor. She desperately tried not to let it show on her face, but he took one look and nodded.

"I wondered if you would figure it out."

"Once you said that, it was a little hard not to. That jealousy is hard to hide."

"I'm not hiding it at all," he argued, with a grin in her direction. "I'm quite delighted to realize he'll pay and suffer for this one."

"Ah, but doesn't it matter that I'll also pay and suffer?"

"No, it doesn't. Sorry about that," he said, with a cheerful grin. "I can't be bothered feeling sorry for you. I have to be focused on saving my own ass."

"When Tristan figures it out, he'll come after you in a big way."

"He might," the man admitted, "but, if I'm not here, he can't do anything." Then he shoved her again, ... hard. She toppled to the ground, as he started swearing again.

"Get your ass up and get moving."

She struggled to her feet, but the fall had her head hurting, and it wasn't hard to make it seem like she was a little worse off than she was. If he kept knocking her around like that, she wouldn't make it very far, and that's what she told him. "Keep hitting me like that, and I'll end up so damaged you won't even get your payday for me."

"Come to think of it, nobody ever told me that there would be no payout if you were dead."

"But they want the damn key, and, if I'm dead, I'll be no help at all in that regard."

He shrugged. "Why the hell they even want that freaking key, I don't even know."

"Because it's full of blackmail material," she stated. "I'm surprised you would even hand it over."

"I don't have it, remember? You have more pull than I do in that direction," he said dismissively.

"Jeez, I don't have any pull," she cried out. "Where did you get that idea?"

He shrugged. "It doesn't matter."

"The hell it doesn't," she snapped. "You're delivering me to somebody who expects me to have something, but I don't have it, and I don't have access to it."

"Maybe so," he conceded, "but what you do have is the

ability to lie and to charm your way out of this, so I'll trust you can do that."

"Otherwise you're totally okay with selling me out to the butchers, is that it?"

He hesitated and shrugged. "Under normal circumstances I would never do something like this, but this isn't normal circumstances. I need to leave town, and this'll be the only way I can get out. Sorry, but tag, and you're it."

She stared at him. "You did something wrong in your job, didn't you?"

"No, I sure didn't," he snapped, "not that I would tell you anyway—just on the off chance that Tristan does find you again, and you would blab your damn mouth right off."

"I sure would," she stated, with a smile. "Everybody would. Here is a guy who's supposedly in a position of trust, but look at you. Look what you've become. Your mama would be very sad."

"You leave my mama out of this," he snapped, glaring at her.

"Why? You think she won't find out about it?"

"Doesn't matter if she does. She wouldn't think anything of it."

"Oh, so her little boy can do no wrong, is that it?" She sneered. "Just a nice little mama's boy, so the whole world owes you a favor, and it doesn't matter that you are now a piece of shit. Nothing but the best for her little boy."

He glared at her, right before he cuffed her hard across the head. She dropped to the floor. He swore again. "Get up," he roared. "Get your ass up." Panic was starting to set in as he realized how much time had gone by.

When a shout came from behind him, he froze and turned. "You fucking bitch," he roared.

She groaned, still on the floor. "What have I got to do with this?"

"You couldn't even walk fast enough to get out of here and to save your own ass, could you?"

"You mean, save *your* ass," she corrected, giving him a hard gaze. "Sorry if I didn't understand the rules of prisoner 101," she snapped, glaring at him.

"The rules of being a kidnapper allow me to do a hell of a lot more than your fucking rules would," he roared again, as he bent down to grab her. When he tried to pick her up, she sagged like a sack of potatoes.

"Stop that," he cried out in frustration. "Don't you understand they're coming?"

"Yeah, of course I understand they're coming." She snorted, looking at him in disbelief. "Why the hell do you think I'm not being very cooperative? You think I want to go to your highest bidder?"

"No, no, no, you don't understand. I can't get caught."

"Yeah, right, … just imagine if your poor old mama found out," she said in a mocking tone.

"Stop that," he growled. "Just stop it."

"Right, as if I'm supposed to help you out."

He dragged her down the hallway, and she let him. It was a whole lot easier to be dragged than to be carried with her head throbbing like it was. However, he wouldn't get very far pulling her like that. When another shout came, this time sounding closer behind them, Amarylis suggested, "You probably should just run. Leave me where I am and go."

"No way. You'll give me up in seconds."

"Of course I will," she retorted. "It's not as if you've treated me well or that I have any sympathy for you." She laughed. "And you also know how Tristan will feel when he finds you."

He nervously looked at the exit door.

"You better go," she urged. "You know the guys on the other side might have something to say to you too."

He glared at her. "Why couldn't you just cooperate?"

She carefully shook her head. "Because I want to live, and you? Well, … obviously you want me dead."

"No, I don't."

"You must because you got into this bullshit, and no way you did it without knowing what the game truly was. Now you get to choose. You get to run and have a chance to get away, or you don't run in time. I hate to say it, but Tristan will take one look at me and … he won't leave any revenge for anybody else." Her captor stared down at her, and she nodded. "He doesn't like it when people mistreat me."

He roared suddenly, frustration and anger flooding through him. "Don't you understand that man's psychotic?"

"Tristan? No, he's not psychotic at all," she argued, "but *you* are. You're the one who's taken all these chances and made a mess of your life." She grimaced. "He's not responsible for this. You don't see him kidnaping a doctor, dragging her down the hallway."

He stared at her, looked down at his hands, then back at her. "God damn it."

"Exactly. Look at what you've done. Look at what you've become."

"No, no, no, no, no," he wailed. "I can't fail at this. You don't understand."

"Oh, I do understand your personality," she stated, determined to drive home the points that were obviously helping. "Yet it doesn't matter what I believe because your mother will find out too. The whole base will eventually hear about you. Once Tristan finds out, absolutely no way he'll let you off."

Her captor shuddered. "He's nuts."

"No, he's not, but he might be a little bit more … concerned with certain things, like people who mistreat me," she pointed out, with a wry smile. "I have to admit it is nice to have somebody who gives a shit and not just some Neanderthal who drags you down a hallway."

He stared at her in shock and shook his head. "Just get up, get up, get up!" She slowly got to her feet, as he half picked her up and half dragged her into an upright position. "Now walk, do you hear me? I will hit you until you walk."

"Do you honestly think hitting me will help me walk?" She stared at him in amazement.

Immediately he belted her across the face again. Her feet fell out from under her, and she collapsed back down again. She stared at him. "That was productive."

"Get up," he cried out in frustration.

"No, I can't get up right now. As soon as I do get up, you will hit me again," she shared, "so I will stay down here."

His frustration boiled over, and he started screaming at her. "Get up, you stupid fucking bitch! Get up!" She just stayed there on the floor, watching the man come completely apart, knowing that Tristan was on his way.

As she refused to cooperate, her captor got more and more out of control, hitting and slapping her. She waited, enduring the pain—leaning into the hits or whatever the hell Jasper had shared with her before—as she watched her captor unravel further and further, to the point that she almost felt sorry for him. When the door opened behind him, and somebody raced to them, she held up her hands, looked at her kidnapper, and said weakly, "I guess it's time to stop now."

He looked at her in shock. "You will get up and walk now then?" he asked hopefully.

"No, I won't get up and walk now," she replied. "Tristan and Jasper are here, and they will take you away now."

He looked at the two men and cried out, "Don't hurt me. Don't hurt me."

Tristan came to her side, the fury in his gaze slowly growing as he studied her face.

"You are the better man, remember that," she whispered to Tristan.

HE SWALLOWED AND took another look at her marred face. "I'm so sorry, Amarylis," he whispered.

She stroked his cheek and gave him a small smile.

Tristan turned the man in front of them. "Morgan, I didn't want to believe it. Of all the people here, I didn't want to believe it was you."

"That's because you wanted to believe it was Sam."

"I did," he confirmed.

"Sam makes it easy to hate him. He's all temper and stupidity," Morgan whispered. Sitting on the floor now, he wrapped his arms around himself and whispered, "I'm not like that."

"Not usually, unfortunately you crossed the line tonight, and that won't go well for you."

Slowly standing up, he nodded. "It's her though," he said, looking at Amarylis. "She wouldn't cooperate."

Amarylis looked over at Tristan and nodded. "He's

right," she stated philosophically. "I wouldn't cooperate. He planned to use the money he sold me for to get out of town. I can see why he might want to leave, but I don't think anyone is outside waiting to pay him."

Morgan frowned at her. "Why not?"

"Because I'm pretty sure whoever is out there has a bullet with your name on it, not any money."

"No, no, no, you don't understand. He's just outside this door." Morgan walked closer to the door. She cried out for him to stop, and he just held up a hand. "I hear you, but I can prove it."

"If you go out that door, you will get shot," she repeated. "And I've got five dead bodies in the morgue to prove it."

"No," he argued, regaining some of his bravado of earlier. "You don't understand how this group works."

"I sure don't," Tristan noted, glancing at Jasper in disbelief. "And the fact that you're even caught up in it is upsetting enough. Did you ever figure out who's behind it all?"

Morgan shook his head. "No, they approached me about getting the damn key." He waved his hand in the general direction of the jail cells in their department.

Tristan nodded. *Tony, aka Terry.*

"I didn't know anything about where the key went, but I had access to her, and that was good enough for them. I even hired someone to get after finding the key, to look for it, but she was always the backup plan. They figured, in the end, she would tell them."

"She won't tell them where it is because she doesn't know where it is," Tristan stated.

Morgan was stunned. "You don't know?" he asked Amarylis.

"I told you that very clearly."

He looked at her and nodded, almost a formal acknowledgment of defeat. He walked toward the door. "Maybe you can catch them, Tristan," he said, suddenly looking fatigued. "Maybe you can put a stop to all of this."

"Did they blackmail you?" Tristan asked, trying to figure out why Morgan would do this.

"They didn't blackmail me," he stated, shaking his head. "I just wanted out, out of it all. When you and Jasper and the others showed up, I knew the handwriting was on the wall." And, with that, he suddenly walked to the door and opened it. He smiled back at them. "See? No bullet." And stepped outside.

And then came a *pop*, and blood burst from his head. He slowly sagged against the door and slipped to the ground.

TRISTAN WALKED BACK over to where Amarylis was sitting up now and talking to Jasper. She looked up at him and smiled. "I'm fine, and he didn't hurt me, not that much. He was mostly frustrated and angry because he wasn't a killer at heart," she shared.

Shaking his head, Tristan gently picked her up and wrapped her up in his arms. "But it could have gone the other way."

"It could have," she admitted, "but it didn't."

"From now on," he promised, "I will bundle you up in Bubble Wrap and keep you there for the rest of the year."

She laughed. "How about you just find the guy who hired Morgan? Well, the big boss behind it all."

"Wouldn't that be nice?" he quipped.

"You've still got those three in the jail cell," she reminded him, "so you are way ahead. From what Morgan told me, he was the one who was after me, so I should be safe now."

"I can't take that chance," he muttered. "We still have too many unanswered questions, so you're going into protective custody."

Patting him on the cheek, she smiled. "Do I get to have a say in this?"

"No, you don't," he declared, as he stared at her, the horror of what could have happened still evident in his face. "I couldn't take it if something had happened to you," he whispered, as he clutched her tightly against his chest.

She melted into him, holding him close, after seeing the depths of his fear and panic. Jasper had a team already racing toward them. "I should work the scene," she muttered.

"You can't," Jasper declared, looking at her with half a smile. "I get that you want to, but that won't happen, and it's not something that Dr. Cox would even allow."

She groaned. "No, he wouldn't, and you're right. My work on a crime scene involving me would compromise the case."

Jasper nodded. "Thank you. Now I'll get you a ride home, and, yes, as Tristan has already told you, you'll be under protection for a while, until we can get to the bottom of this, but the good news is we're slowly unraveling the data to date."

"Are you?" she asked, with an odd look.

He smiled and nodded. "Yes, we are."

"And what about Mason? How is he doing?"

"He's been conscious a little bit, although I haven't managed to catch him while he's been awake." Jasper sighed. "We do have several women under protective custody right now, and I know that you don't want to hear this, but you will need to join them." She glared at him, and he nodded. "My partner, Master's partner, Gideon's partner, and now you, Tristan's partner," he shared, with an exasperated tone.

She was gearing up to retort, but Jasper held up a hand. "No arguments. Tristan will take you there himself, after we get you checked out at the hospital, then back at your place to pack up whatever you need. Make sure you take enough for a few days. … That's *not* negotiable."

When she growled in frustration, Jasper nodded. "Your job will keep, and, in spite of all this craziness, we'll make sure you're still alive at the end of it."

She groaned again. Then Tristan snatched her up in his arms again and held her close. "Fine," she whispered, "but I'll have you know it's not my normal way."

Tristan faced her and grinned. "We saw that today. Now let's run by the hospital, then get you packed up and on the road. We'll take a pit stop at my place to eat and relax."

"I wish I could stay at your place."

"If we could find a guard, then that's possible. As it is stands right now, we need to maximize our manpower and resources, and gather our people under a shared guard or two."

CHAPTER 13

AMARYLIS WALKED INTO his place, dumped her overnight bag at the front door, and turned to face him. He'd barely dropped his keys on the side table when she launched herself into his arms. "Are you sure I can't stay here?" She placed her hands on either side of his face and kissed him with such longing and passion that she felt his knees buckle.

She didn't know about him, but she needed this. She needed to know that those close calls were over and that she was safe and that he was here with her—as he'd been every step of the way. She didn't know when she'd started to care but suspected when he'd first walked into her office. So capable. So in command. Who knew power was so sexy? And so was self-confidence. Something he had in spades.

The room tilted as she was lifted and suddenly found herself carried down the hallway to a bedroom, where she was placed gently onto a huge bed. She scrambled to her knees and laughed when she saw him pulling his T-shirt over his head. She was stripped in seconds and kneeling on the bed, wearing just her tiny thong.

He froze, a look of wonder on his face. "Oh dear God," he whispered, almost in prayer.

She grinned and cupped her breasts. "Like what you see?"

"Love it, but love what's inside that beautiful packaging even more," he whispered, as he slowly knelt on the bed beside her, reaching around her, sliding his hands down her back to cup her butt and to pull her tightly against his erection. "And that packaging is something else too …"

She laughed and collapsed backward, pulling him on top of her. "We need this," she stated, without giving him any chance to argue, although arguing was the last thing on his mind. She planted another deep tongue-warring kiss on him before he took over and kissed her with a tongue-plunging movement that matched his hips, sending her temperature soaring. She didn't want it to go too fast, but she'd been the driving force behind this so …

Opening her thighs, she cried out as he slid to her entrance and stalled there, as she lay trembling, … waiting. When he held back, she wrapped her legs around his hips and plunged upward, crying out as he went deep inside her.

He froze.

"I'm fine," she cried out. "I'm fine. God, don't stop."

He lowered his head and buried his face in her hair, then slid his hands down her back to hold her hips and started to move.

She cried out in joy. She cried in tears. Then she cried out as her climax ripped through her. She sagged back to the bed, and he pumped once, twice, then roared as he spent himself deep inside her. Finally he stretched out beside her, tucking her up close. She loved hearing his ragged breathing, his gasps for air. His massive chest rose unevenly beneath her ear.

"Dear Lord, you're killing me," he murmured.

"I don't think you're that delicate," she noted, chuckling, lifting to look up at him, "but I didn't want that to be over so quickly."

"Neither did I," he admitted. "Give me a minute."

"And we can go again?" she asked, with a grin of delight. She laughed when he nodded. She relaxed back down, absolutely loving where they were at, all the peace, quiet, and loving togetherness. It didn't get better than this.

After a moment, opening his eyes, Tristan tucked her closer beside him and whispered, "I don't know about you, but I think this little road trip to the safe house has been pretty great so far," he teased.

She sighed. "I just … I don't want to leave everything behind. Like you."

"I will come and visit," he shared. "I just don't know how often I'll get that opportunity."

"Plus, who knows what else will happen between now and then?"

"Nothing that'll put you in danger," he declared. "Not again."

She reached up and kissed him deeply, adding, "That's all fine, but what about you? No point in looking after me if it means you're not there at the end of the day."

He rolled over, pulled her up close again, and whispered, "I'll be there."

"Are you sure?"

"I'm sure."

"Promise?"

He chuckled. "I promise."

And she knew such a promise was silly, but somehow it still made her feel so much better. She nodded. "In that case," she murmured, as she rolled over slowly, now sitting astride him. "Maybe we have a few more minutes before we start this next stage of our lives."

He reached up, cupping her breasts, and murmured, "I like the sound of that, but this is just a prelude. The next stage of our lives will be you and me together." He hesitated. "If that's okay with you?"

"It's better than okay," she declared, looking at him in delight. "It's absolutely perfect. I can't think of anything I would like better." She leaned over and kissed him. "Just in case you're in doubt …" She lowered her head again, making sure no doubts were left, … for either of them.

This concludes Book 4 of Man Down: Tristan.
Read about Guilliam: Man Down, Book 5

Man Down: Guilliam (Book #5)

There is no greater motive than bloodlust, DNA, and revenge mixed up in a cocktail of hatred ...

Guilliam watched his long term relationship dissolve and to a certain extent he understood it. He knew when the time was right, he'd try again. He didn't expect to see her immediately upon arrival at the hospital though as he joined Jasper's investigation team.

Janelle walked away from Guilliam to nurse her sick mother. It was supposed to be temporary but the cancer was deadly and she was staying in the hospital room knowing it was her mother's last few weeks. Finding out Guilliam was there helped, but knowing he was involved in something deadly had her feeling like she was being watched all the time.

It takes everyone to get to the bottom of this nightmare, but not before it gets way worse…

GUILLIAM LAFRANKO STEPPED into the hospital and located the room number Tesla had given him. He made an ever-so-slight knock before stepping inside.

She looked up, blanked out for just a moment, then stood up and threw her arms around him. "You came," she cried out.

He hugged her closely. "Of course I did," he murmured, as he looked over at the friend he'd known for so long and sighed. "I sure don't enjoy seeing him like this."

"He won't enjoy you seeing him like this either," she admitted.

"Understood," Guilliam replied, with a nod. "Warriors should always be on their feet, never like this." He looked back at her and asked, "The men, have they found anything?"

"Lots," she admitted, "just not enough."

"It's always that way," he noted. "I'll go find them."

"I haven't told them you were coming."

He waved his hand. "I contacted Jasper, so he knows I'm here."

"Oh good, I wasn't sure how he would take it."

"It doesn't matter how he takes it," he replied, smiling at her. "All that matters is that we get the job done." He took another close look at his longtime friend Mason and asked, "He's conscious, no?"

"He has been, yes. He manages a few minutes, recognizes me, then goes back under."

"That's good," he noted. "You don't want to push him for more than that right now. If he understood what was going on out here, he would fight to stay conscious, and then he wouldn't heal."

She stared at Guilliam and then nodded. "That's very true. I have to remember that."

"You need to temporarily look after yourself, the baby, and Sebastian, without Mason's help, while Mason looks after himself, despite his condition."

"I hear you," she muttered. "It's just been so terribly hard to sit here and to wait."

"It won't be much longer," he stated. "Hopefully we'll solve this before he wakes up permanently." He gave her a gentle hug and a kiss on the cheek. "You stay here, where it's safe."

"How did you get past the guard?"

"The guard knows me," he said, with a smile, "at least he did once he recognized me. Most people don't recognize me right off the bat. I do that on purpose, but I knew who the guard was on duty right now, so it's all good."

"As long as nobody else can pull that trick."

"No, nobody else will pull that trick. I promise. Do you need anything?"

"No," she whispered, her voice wavering a bit, as she touched her swollen belly. "I just need Mason back."

"He's alive. He's fighting to come back to you. He's waking up occasionally to remind us that he's still in there, fighting. Solving the case and keeping everybody safe in the meantime is up to us."

She nodded. "Do you need anything?"

He smiled. "No, I'm fine." Then studying her for a moment, he asked, "What's up, Tesla?"

She hesitated. "It's just that … Janelle is here."

He raised an eyebrow, as he contemplated Tesla. "Looking after Mason?"

"No, it's her mother. She's a patient here and in a pretty bad way."

He froze, and a sad look entered his gaze. "I'm so sorry to hear that. … Janelle's always been very close to her mother."

"And to you," Tesla pointed out.

"And to me," he confirmed, "but it just wasn't our time. This isn't the time either," he stated, looking at her sternly. "No matchmaking."

She smiled. "I'm not matchmaking. I'm just telling you that she's here, in case you want to see her."

"I'll see," he replied. "Is she working here at this hospital?"

"Sometimes. She comes and goes."

"Of course, and her mom is here?"

Tesla shrugged. "She is. It sounds serious, as if she may not have too long."

He winced. "All right, I'll, … I'll see about contacting her." As he walked away from Tesla and Mason, Guilliam knew he couldn't see Janelle—or her mother. If ever you had loved and lost that one special woman in your life, you sure as hell didn't want to go through such pain again. As he headed down the hallway to the stairs, a woman called out to him.

"Guilliam?"

He froze and turned to look, as Janelle walked toward him. "Janelle," he said, with a smile. "How are you?"

"I'm fine. How are you?" Her words were barely more than a whisper, and her face was pale with shock. "I never expected to see you."

"I can't say that I planned to be here, but *Mason*," he said, with a nod toward his room.

She winced and nodded. "That makes sense. If ever somebody would bring you back here, it would be him."

He hesitated before he added, "Tesla told me about your mother."

Janelle stiffened at first, then slowly relaxed. "Honestly, at this point, her passing will be a blessing," she admitted. "Watching her suffer is pretty hard to take, but it won't be long now."

"I'm so sorry."

She shrugged. "It will be a good thing for Mom."

"In that case, ... I hope for an easy passing," he said, as he inched away.

As she headed toward her mother's room, avoiding any more discussion with Guilliam, she called back, "Were you going to contact me?"

He looked up at her and schooled his features. "I just got here. I didn't know you were here, not until Tesla mentioned it."

"Your head may not have known," she stated, "but your heart would have."

And, with that comment, he knew that any pretense would be completely useless. "I might have looked you up once I realized just what the lay of the land was. My first focus has been on Mason."

"Of course," she replied, a little more formally. "Still, if you can spare a few minutes at some point, it would be nice to spend some time with you."

He stiffened, knowing that spending time with her, although it was everything he'd always wanted, would also be terribly painful for him to endure.

She cut away his unspoken protest and added, "A lot of heartache remains between us, but I would very much like to heal that pain."

He groaned. "I'm not sure that healing for you is the same as for me."

"Maybe not," she whispered, "but it might help us both to spend some time together to find out."

He searched her features. "This is new territory for me, so I don't know what to say."

She nodded. "Me too. Nothing like watching somebody dying to make you realize that other decisions you've made may not have been the best." He winced at that, and she nodded. "I hurt you, and I didn't mean to, and I hurt myself as well," she admitted, with a sigh. "I thought I was doing the right thing because my mother needed me."

"She did need you," he confirmed, "and, of course, you had to come help her."

"I did, and you're right, but I didn't have to tear apart what we had. I, … I don't know what I was thinking or why I did what I did."

His phone went off at that moment, like a lifesaver, and he nodded. "We'll talk. Beyond that, no promises. I have to go."

And, with that, he bolted down the stairs to get out of the hospital and to get away from his past as quickly as he could. One thing he had learned a long time ago was that you could never go back to the way things had been before. Still, a tiny voice in the back of his head whispered that maybe he didn't have to go back to that. Maybe, just maybe, something better was ahead.

Find Book 5 here!

To find out more visit Dale Mayer's website.

https://geni.us/DMSMDGuilliam

Author's Note

Thank you for reading Tristan: Man Down, Book 4! If you enjoyed the book, please take a moment and leave a short review.

Dear reader,

I love to hear from readers, and you can contact me at my website: www.dalemayer.com or at my Facebook author page. To be informed of new releases and special offers, sign up for my newsletter or follow me on BookBub. And if you are interested in joining Dale Mayer's Reader Group, here is the Facebook sign up page.
http://geni.us/DaleMayerFBGroup

Cheers,
Dale Mayer

About the Author

Dale Mayer is a *USA Today* best-selling author, best known for her SEALs military romances, her Psychic Visions series, and her Lovely Lethal Garden cozy series. Her contemporary romances are raw and full of passion and emotion (Broken But ... Mending, Hathaway House series). Her thrillers will keep you guessing (Kate Morgan, By Death series), and her romantic comedies will keep you giggling (*It's a Dog's Life*, a stand-alone novella; and the Broken Protocols series, starring Charming Marvin, the cat).

Dale honors the stories that come to her—and some of them are crazy, break all the rules and cross multiple genres!

To go with her fiction, she also writes nonfiction in many different fields, with books available on résumé writing, companion gardening, and the US mortgage system. All her books are available in print and ebook format.

Connect with Dale Mayer Online

Dale's Website – www.dalemayer.com

Twitter – @DaleMayer

Facebook Page – geni.us/DaleMayerFBFanPage

Facebook Group – geni.us/DaleMayerFBGroup

BookBub – geni.us/DaleMayerBookbub

Instagram – geni.us/DaleMayerInstagram

Goodreads – geni.us/DaleMayerGoodreads

Newsletter – geni.us/DaleNews